Praise for the *Wimpy Vampire* series by Tim Collins

'This series of vampire parodies is one of the
funniest I've ever read.'
wondrousreads.com

'Fantastically witty and hugely entertaining, this fun
and accessible diary will appeal to any fan of *Twilight* or
Adrian Mole, teenage or otherwise...'
Goodreads.com

'*Twilight* meets *Diary of a Wimpy Kid* in this
inventive parody of both.'
guardianbookshop.co.uk

'This hilarious book will have you laughing your head off as
you learn of the misfortune of Nigel Mullet.'
Fresh Direction

'Teens who are fans of the *Twilight* saga will love
this laugh-out-loud parody.'
Woman's Way

'A funny light-hearted read which touches on first love.'
Books 4 Teens

Diary
of a
Grumpy
Old Git

Tim Collins

Diary of a Grumpy Old Git

Getting through life one rant at a time

Michael O'Mara Books Limited

First published in Great Britain in 2012 by
Michael O'Mara Books Limited
9 Lion Yard
Tremadoc Road
London SW4 7NQ

A CIP catalogue record for this book is available from the British Library.

Papers used by Michael O'Mara Books Limited are natural,
recyclable products made from wood grown in sustainable forests.
The manufacturing processes conform to the environmental
regulations of the country of origin.

ISBN: 978-1-84317-991-7 in hardback print format
ISBN: 978-1-84317-979-5 in EPub format
ISBN: 978-1-84317-980-1 in Mobipocket format

1 2 3 4 5 6 7 8 9 10

Designed and typeset by Envy Design
Illustrations by Andrew Pinder

Printed and bound by CPI Group (UK) Ltd, Croydon, CR0 4YY

www.mombooks.com

Acknowledgements
Thanks to Louise Dixon, Andrew Pinder, Collette
Collins and everyone at Michael O'Mara books.

TUESDAY 1ST JANUARY

Apparently I'm a grumpy old git. I must be, because someone bought me this diary in the office Secret Santa. It has the words 'Grumpy Old Git' on the cover, alongside a picture of a scowling man.

At first I wondered if someone had given it to me by mistake. Even if I were to accept I was grumpy, I'd have a problem with the 'old' bit. How can I be over the hill already? I wasn't even old enough to be a proper punk, though I did wear a safety pin through my school tie and I spat on Trevor Chalkley once. But everyone spat on Trevor Chalkley. It doesn't really count.

You know what I would have bought for me? A copy of *Home Alone*. Why not? Everyone knows about Sarah leaving. Might as well joke about it.

Anyway, I got this diary, so I suppose I should make an effort to use it. I'm not expecting much to happen to me, but at least I've completed the first page. Who knows? I might actually stick with it. There's a first time for everything.

WEDNESDAY 2ND JANUARY

I don't want to be a grumpy old git. It's not that I think there's anything wrong with being dour, I just don't want to fit a demographic. I'm going to prove whoever bought me this diary wrong by remaining cheerful and upbeat for a whole year. It can't be difficult. The years are going by so fast now that it hardly seems like a challenge at all.

I'm going to start thinking about pleasant things right now.

The innocent laughter of children.
There. No arguing with that. Although when I think back to childhood, the sort of things we were laughing about weren't really that innocent. For example, we used to wipe the blackboard eraser on the front of Trevor Chalkley's trousers and call him 'Chalky Balls'. I can remember giggling a lot over that one. So next time you hear the echo of distant playground laughter, remember that it's probably directed at some lonely child who smells of milk.

A basket full of fluffy kittens.
Aww, just look at them. Aren't they cute? Although they only evolved to look cute so we'd feed them and they wouldn't have to hunt. We give them food, we give them warmth, we give them shelter and in return they show us their anuses whenever we try and stroke them. Basket of kittens? Basket of rude, manipulative, freeloading bastards, more like.

A beautiful sunrise.

Yep, just look at that lovely sun. The same sun that will one day explode, farting out waves of gas that will consume and destroy the earth. In the meantime, it peeks above the horizon like a leering psychopath. *I'm going to destroy you one day*, it says. *But for now I'll let you live.*

To tell you the truth I've seen more than enough sodding sunrises recently, as I haven't been sleeping well. I thought I'd get eight or nine hours a night without Sarah digging me in the ribs for snoring, but now I wake up at four every morning for a bout of pathetic worrying. It's like I've got some sort of internal radio alarm that wakes me up with the voice of deep existential dread. You're listening to Ennui FM, where we play nothing but the fundamental pointlessness of existence.

OK, I might need a bit of practice at this whole positivity thing. But I'm sure I can manage it. As long as I believe in myself, I can complete this extraordinary journey, or whatever they say on those talent shows.

THURSDAY 3RD JANUARY

I woke up early again this morning. I turned on the radio in an effort to drown out my usual aimless worrying. It turns out that the radio is even more depressing than my usual aimless worrying.

How does music manage to keep getting worse? When Duran Duran and Spandau Ballet were parading around with their eye shadow and tea towels, we all thought it was a travesty, like punk had never happened. But they're Mozart compared to the atrocities I heard this morning. Will this keep happening? What could possibly come next that will make today's pop sound good? Will the sound of someone scraping their nails down a blackboard get to number one? Because it's the only thing that would sound worse than that autotuned crap they were playing this morning.

I'm aware of the standard reply to all this, by the way. *You're not meant to get it. You're too old. Your parents didn't like the music you played when you were a teenager.*

But our parents hated our music because it was too noisy, too new, too frightening. I hate today's stuff because it's too crap. You can't just like crap and pretend we're too old to understand it. That's cheating.

Friday 4th January

A new woman called Jen started at the office today. She has long brown hair and blue eyes and looks like a younger, prettier version of Sarah. As I watched her from my desk at the back of the office, I imagined us going out to poncy restaurants together, enjoying long country walks and getting tagged in pictures on Facebook that Sarah would see.

Later in the morning I spoke to her and she turned out to be one of those people who make every sentence sound like a question. She also described herself as 'proactive' and a 'self-starter' even though she wasn't in a job interview. Then she said she thought our company was going to be a 'totes amazeballs' place to work.

So long, Jen. It's a shame it couldn't last, but I'll never forget those precious few moments between when I saw you and when you spoke.

Saturday 5th January
Today I'm going to train myself to be more cheerful by repeating positive thoughts.

The glass is half full.
Half full of what? Vomit? Poison? Bacardi Breezer? I might want it to be empty.

Turn that frown upside down.
Would this actually make someone look like they were smiling? Wouldn't you just look like you had a disturbing upside-down mouth? Or one of those people who grin but have sad eyes that show they're actually dying inside?

It takes more muscles to frown than to smile.
But using muscles is a good thing, isn't it? That's why people pay hundreds of pounds for gym memberships they can't bring themselves to cancel.

If someone tells me that it takes more muscles to frown than to smile, I like to raise my hand and extend my middle finger. It uses fewer muscles than either, and is a far more appropriate response.

When life gives you lemons, make lemonade.
I remember the time I tried to make lemonade. I got as far as twisting a lemon on the squeezer when a painful jet of juice squirted into my eye. I spent the next few minutes groping around in the bathroom for my Optrex and plastic eyebath. Then I gave up and sat on the edge of my bed, weeping silently until the pain went away. So rather than interpret this phrase as 'make the best of a bad situation', I interpret it as 'sit on the edge of the bed and snivel pathetically when you're in a bad situation'.

Follow your dreams.
Which dreams? What about the dream where I turn up to work with no pants on? Would you like me to follow that?

Your prayers will be answered.
Why would anyone think this is a comforting thing to say? It doesn't say what the answer will be. It's a bit like saying, 'Your request for an overdraft extension will be answered.' It doesn't mean you'll get what you want.

You can't have a rainbow without a little rain.
I don't mind a spot of rain every now and then, and I'm sick of everyone from songwriters to weather forecasters assuming otherwise. Rainbows, on the other hand, I can take or leave. I don't even bother getting my camera phone out for them any more.

At least I'm not trapped in the wreckage of a car and blacking out from blood loss as I cry for help.
I made this one up myself and it's unlikely to feature on a motivational poster anytime soon, but it was the only uplifting motto I couldn't find fault with.

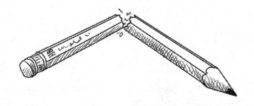

19

Sunday 6th January

The kitchen stool broke today. In the old days, this would have meant a drive to Ikea, an interminable trudge around the store's one-way system and a feeble afternoon of trying to work out how a pile of wood, screws and Allen keys relates to the assembly diagram.

But now? I simply force the broken chair into my wheelie bin and eat my Alpen standing up. Sarah can make Brad troop around that Nordic hell if she likes. I'm free now.

Did I mention that Sarah's new boyfriend is called Brad? He would be, wouldn't he? When fate plays that sort of joke on you, it's best to laugh along. Let it know it's got to you and it will only make things worse. Like he'll turn out to be an estate agent or something.

Monday 7th January

My boss Steve briefed me to write a brochure for a new
street-sweeping machine today. It needs to be 2,000
words long and I've got a week to do it. I thought it
might take three hours, so I asked for an extra couple
of weeks.

The project is so dull that no one else will want
anything to do with it, and I should be able to drag it
out for ages before anyone chases it up.

When I got fired from my ad agency in the mid-nineties, I asked the headhunter for the least desirable job she had, so I could get away with doing as little as possible without any swotty grads snapping at my heels. She suggested this industrial copywriting job, and I've been here ever since.

The first few years went fairly slowly, but in 1999 I got Internet access on my desktop and it's been fine thereafter. I just have to work a few hours every week, and pretend forklift trucks and road sweepers are fascinating whenever I'm dragged into a meeting, and I get to spend the rest of my time faffing around on YouTube and iTunes. Bliss.

Hang on a minute, I just said something positive! And I wasn't even trying! See? I'm not a grumpy old git at all! I'm a grinning happy-clappy old git! Hallelujah!

TUESDAY 8TH JANUARY

I went to Starbucks this lunchtime. I usually avoid asking the assistants for anything other than a cup of coffee, but today I asked if I could 'get' a 'venti caramel macchiato'. I even said 'pain au chocolate' in a slight French accent. I felt capable of anything after that.

I had my eye on one of the leather sofas, but a man with ginger dreadlocks barged in and reserved it with his rucksack before getting in the queue behind me. If you're going to be this rude, why queue at all? Why not push right in front of me? In fact, why not grab the caramel macchiato out of my hand while you're at it?

In the end, I had to sit down at a messy table and listen to the ginger Bob Marley phoning his friends, who all seemed to be called 'dude' and 'buddy'. But it didn't bother me because I'm not grumpy any more. I know it might have looked like I crushed my paper cup and ground my teeth until I burst a blood vessel in my eye, but that was just an illusion.

Wednesday 9th January

Jen sits over at the front of the office, so I can't tell exactly what she's up to, but I think she keeps finishing her work early and asking for more. I know it sounds crazy, but I can't think of any other explanation. She's always printing things out and taking them to Steve's office. I mentioned this to Imran and Cathy, who sit next to me at the back, and they were suitably horrified.

I suggested that one of them should have a word with her about it, but they weren't interested.

Jen is exactly the sort of workaholic I was trying to avoid by coming here. You'd think someone who wants to do crazy things like come in early and finish their projects before the deadline could find somewhere better to work. Yet all it takes is a recession and a scarcity of jobs, and suddenly you're overrun with latte-drinking zombies bleating about their proactivity. I think I even heard Jen refer to Steve as 'team leader' this afternoon. I must have been imagining it. No one can be that annoying.

Tonight I wheeled my bin down to the front of the driveway for collection and I noticed I was the only person who wasn't chucking out a mountain of shiny Christmas tat. I felt grateful for my freedom from Sarah once again. This was the first year I didn't have to bother with decorations and it was a huge relief. No covering the front of the house with tacky lights to compete with the neighbours, no treading pine needles into the carpet and no spotting tiny scraps of tinsel still stuck to the ceiling in the middle of June.

And what do we get for coating every visible surface with sparkly rubbish? The chance to say we feel 'all

Christmassy'. What does this even mean? Is it a distinct emotion like happiness or sadness? Do people feel it in summer by mistake and have to drink Pimm's and listen to the Beach Boys until it passes?

Anyway, except for asking for turkey instead of chicken in Subway, I made no attempt whatsoever to celebrate Christmas this year, and I didn't miss it one bit.

Thursday 10th January

My train was delayed this morning because of 'signal failure.' It always seems to be signal failure. Either they need to stop buying their signals from the pound shop or this is just a vaguely technical excuse they trot out when their staff are too hungover to show up.

I was forced to get the bus instead. The only free seats downstairs were reserved for infirm or disabled people, so I had to go to the top deck, where a teenage boy with massive headphones was listening to hip hop so loudly we could all hear the rapper boasting about his possessions.

I strolled up to him with every intention of telling him that the music would damage his ears if I didn't get to them first. But then I remembered my vow to be more cheerful. Instead, I asked him what he was listening to and said it sounded really cool. He looked at me with contempt, and he was right to.

The driver waited until I was walking down the stairs before making an emergency stop, which sent me tumbling down to the lower deck. No wonder they need to reserve so many seats for the infirm and disabled. Most regular bus users probably end up that way.

When I got into work, I was too traumatized to do anything, so I spent the morning on Facebook. Jen has tagged Brad in a photo now. I clicked through to his profile. It turns out he's an estate agent.

FRIDAY 11TH JANUARY

This is worrying. Steve announced today that we've lost the Donaldson Sweepers account. At first I was pleased because it meant I wouldn't have to write the brochure and I could concentrate on the Scrabble game I've downloaded for my laptop. But then I thought they might have to get rid of someone and it was more likely to be the person who plays board games all day than the person who finishes their work early and asks for more.

My fear was compounded when Steve popped over to my desk on his way out and said we should catch up first thing on Monday as there was 'something we need to discuss'.

You can't do that. You can't just say there's 'something we need to discuss' and swan off for the weekend. What am I supposed to do now? This was going to be the weekend I finally got round to my *Sopranos* box set. There's no way I'll be able to focus on it now.

Saturday 12th January

I had another peek at Brad's Facebook profile today. He seems to be one of those people who can't do anything without posting it for all his friends to see.

These people think we're all wildly impressed with their choice of holidays, restaurants and friends. They don't realize that the only thing they're really communicating is their unhappiness. They're so insecure they need constant validation for everything they ever do from everyone they've ever met. It's like they've never got past that stage of running into the kitchen to show their parents the drawing they did at school today.

Look at me, I'm on holiday. Look at me, I'm out with my friends. Look at me, I'm in a restaurant owned by a TV chef. Look at me, I actually paid money to watch some shitty band in a huge indoor arena.

Well done, you. Let's give you a pat on the head. Let's give you a gold star. Let's stick your entire life up here on the fridge where we'll all be able to see it.

SUNDAY 13TH JANUARY

I notice from Facebook that Brad has taken Sarah to Brussels for the weekend. I'm guessing he takes all his girlfriends there, as it's the only place in the world he's more interesting than.

Look at him with his baseball cap and dark glasses on an overcast day. There he is in front of the Atomium with his jumper draped over his shoulders. I had no idea anyone outside a catalogue actually did that.

Well, guess what, Brad? You were stupid enough to put your email address and mobile number on Facebook, and now I'm going to give you so much spam you'll think I'm a dinner lady from the seventies. Here we go. Would you like text alerts about our great offers? Yes, please. Would you like us to email you with details of our upcoming events? You bet. Please enter the time when you'd like our support staff to call you back. Can you do five on Saturday morning?

What a loser.

I'm sure there are some who'd point out that I'm the one who's just spent an entire weekend looking at someone else's Facebook page, and therefore I'm the actual loser. But at least I found something to take my mind off tomorrow's ominous meeting. So I'm a winner, really.

Monday 14th January

I got in early this morning, as I wanted to be alert and ready to argue back if Steve tried to get rid of me.

I've never been on the early train before. Every carriage was full of neat young men and women sipping skinny lattes and prodding their iPhones. They'd probably already thrown together a PowerPoint presentation, been to the gym and done a charity parachute jump. Now they were racing to their offices to stare smugly at the normal people who stroll blearily in at 9:33. I'm not saying I wanted the train to crash. But if a train had to crash, that's the one I'd pick.

Jen was already sitting behind her desk when I got in. Did she even go home? Or did she stay there all night typing, 'All work and no play makes Jen a dull girl'?

Steve didn't turn up until half nine, and he faffed around in the kitchen for ages, prolonging my torture. It was almost ten by the time he called me into his office to give me the bad news.

At least, the sort of bad news. I haven't been given the sack, but Steve is leaving on Friday, which means I'll have a new boss on Monday.

Eek.

I'm going to get made redundant, aren't I? Everyone knows that new bosses clear out the dead wood. And if anyone around here is shedding bark, covered in fungus and blocking the footpath, it's me.

I don't care if I get made redundant. I'll take a year out to do all the things I've always wanted to do.

But what are all the things I've always wanted to do? I'd quite like to order the fillet steak in Chez Gérard. I've not started on my *Sopranos* box set yet. And the garden could do with some decking. That's pretty much it. It's not going to take a whole year, is it?

Who am I kidding? Of course I don't want to get made redundant. It would be a disaster. I won't even be able to keep up the payments on the ground-floor flat I moved into after the separation from Sarah. I'll be forced to traipse around the streets pushing my identical clothes in a trolley and telling passers-by that I could have been a contender in the world of industrial brochure writing.

I've got to keep my job. I won't get another one. I'll beg if I need to. I'm not proud.

TUESDAY 15TH JANUARY

Cathy and Imran were panicking this morning about how this new boss was going to sack everyone. Jen must have overheard, because she sauntered over and said, 'Don't worry, guys, you'll get on fine with Josh.'

It turns out that Jen has known about this new boss all along, as he interviewed her for the job. So not only is this person called Josh, but he chose Jen over some other candidates. He heard her speaking and he actually chose to be in the same building as her. This doesn't bode well.

My blood didn't really run cold, however, until Jen described him as 'funky'. I can't imagine any description that would have been more disturbing. She could have said he was a keen collector of Nazi memorabilia or an avid badger baiter, and I'd have been less perturbed. I can take a lot of the horrendous things that life throws at me, but I'm not sure a 'funky' boss is one of them.

WEDNESDAY 16TH JANUARY

I must be losing my mind with stress because I apologized to a cyclist this morning. I swerved to avoid the carcass of a bizarre multi-limbed creature that turned out to be an abandoned KFC value meal. This sent me right into the path of an overweight cyclist wearing a pink safety helmet. She slammed her brakes on and tutted loudly, and I muttered 'sorry'.

Why? Why was I sorry that she nearly ran me over on the pavement?

I regained my senses and shouted, 'Actually I'm not sorry at all. You're supposed to be on the road. Just because what you're doing is good for the planet doesn't give you the right to put everyone else at risk. You know what? Get a Land Rover and make the icecaps melt. It would be safer swimming to work than avoiding you bastards.'

The woman didn't hang around to listen. She whizzed off, leaving me ranting into thin air like someone who sits in the park all day drinking Special Brew. Which I probably will be soon.

Thursday 17th January

In these times of crisis what I need is a serene, calm life. Instead, I get an endless parade of trivial frustrations. Today I got stuck behind an old lady at a cashpoint. It's not like I was expecting her to be quick, but the faffing went on so long that anyone's blood would have gone on to an even simmer.

The first thing that pissed me off was her complete lack of preparation. You'd think that someone waiting in the queue for a cashpoint might go to the trouble of getting their card ready. But this old bat actually waited until she read the screen before fishing around in her bag. What was she expecting it to ask her to do? Play 'Axel F' on the keypad?

The woman rooted through her purse and tried four different cash cards. At least, I'm assuming they were cash cards. They could have been library cards for all I know. After several centuries of this, I leant forward and tapped her on the shoulder to let her know there was someone else in the queue. Then the old trout had the cheek to accuse me of trying to 'steal her PIN number'.

I told her that it probably wouldn't be much use to me, as she certainly hadn't managed to produce any cash with it in the last twenty minutes. And anyway, it's called a 'PIN' not a 'PIN number'. What you're effectively saying there is 'Personal Identification Number number'.

You know what I think? I think the old lady didn't even want any cash. I think she just likes to queue. In the unlikely event that one of those cards ever produced cash, she'd be straight down the bank to put it back in her account. And you can bet she'd wait until she got to the window before filling in the slip.

But I resolved to be more positive this year, didn't I? So I should end on a good thing that happened.

Er ... the bank didn't charge me for using the cashpoint. I know this because they told me before returning my card. That was quite good, I suppose. Although I find it very suspicious that banks feel the need to congratulate themselves every time they resist doing something evil. I resisted killing an old lady today, but you don't catch me boasting about it.

FRIDAY 18TH JANUARY

We went down the pub for Steve's leaving drinks tonight. I asked him if he had a new job yet, but he said he was taking early retirement, the utter bastard. Apparently, he's paid off the mortgage on both his houses, so now he can move into one and live off the rent of the other.

It doesn't seem fair really. Just because he's earned loads more money than me and invested it sensibly, he's free to do as he pleases while I remain trapped in a room full of idiots. Someone should give me enough money to retire. I wonder if there are any charities for gits.

Steve left quite soon and the rest of the night was a complete washout. I got trapped talking to Jen about her career ambitions, and I had to pretend I thought they were in some way worthwhile so she wouldn't grass me up to her funky mate Josh.

Saturday 19th January

Another small victory today. I noticed that my chicken tikka masala ready-meal was past its use-by date. But guess what? I ate it anyway. This is something that would never have happened under the Sarah regime. She obeyed use-by dates like they were commands from God, rather than approximate guidelines. She once got out of bed at five past midnight to throw away an iceberg lettuce that had just passed its expiry date.

The moment I knew it was all over for us was when she said our marriage had passed its use-by date. If she'd put it any other way, I might have believed there was a way back. But not that.

Sunday 20th January

I meant to watch my *Sopranos* box set today, but I got distracted by worrying about whether the correct phrase was 'box set' or 'boxed set'. I searched online and 'box set' seems to be standard, but it doesn't sound right to me. It's not a set of boxes, it's a set of items in a box.

Perhaps I should go on some sort of crusade to save the phrase 'boxed set', but it's probably too late. There's no point in trying to save language in a world where bosses can be described as 'funky'. If things have got that bad, we might as well return to pointing and grunting.

I'm going to spend tonight trawling the dark recesses of my imagination to guess what Jen meant by 'funky'. Beards, ponytails, baseball caps – nothing will be taboo. Then however things turn out tomorrow, I'll already have anticipated it. That's the great thing about being a pessimist. You're never disappointed.

Monday 21st January

The newspapers reckon today is the most depressing day of the year. It's called 'Blue Monday' because of some bogus calculation about how bad the weather is likely to be and how little money you're likely to have left.

Actually, I beg to differ. The twenty-fifth of December is the most depressing day of the year. When you're a kid it's depressing because your expectations are so high that only a pair of hover shoes and a working time machine would meet them. And when you're an adult it's depressing because you're drunk and shouting at your relatives before noon. It wasn't depressing for me this year, because I stayed in bed all day. But it has been every other year.

Nonetheless, it all increased my anxiety about meeting Josh. 'Blue Monday' didn't seem like a very good day to meet a new boss.

Josh didn't turn out to be too horrendous, though. There wasn't much interesting about him at all, really. He had short black hair, black trousers and a white shirt that was quite probably tucked into his underpants. The only thing that really caught my attention about him was that **HE LOOKED ABOUT EIGHT YEARS OLD.**

Seriously. I thought a paperboy had sneaked into Steve's old office to see what it was like to sit in a grown-up's chair. But apparently that little foetus is my new boss. I hope he's been through puberty. I don't think I could handle the mood swings.

I'm tempted to find out his actual age, but I'm not sure I want to know. Was he even alive when I saw *Star Wars* in the cinema? Or *Back to the Future*? Or *Jurassic Park*? He probably wasn't even alive when I walked out of *Mamma Mia* because Pierce Brosnan started singing.

Well, now he's my boss and I have to do what he says. So I take back what I said yesterday. Pessimists can be disappointed, too.

Tuesday 22nd January

It looks as though I'm getting the chop after all.

There are a couple of new people joining next week. I only found out because I saw our office manager Erika going round and changing the phone lists. I asked her who Jo and Jez were and she said they were starting on Monday. I asked her where they were going to sit and she said they could perch on the ends of our desks for the time being. *For the time being.* Subtle, eh?

Imran and Cathy immediately started fretting about which of us would be fired to make way for these newcomers. I told them there was probably nothing to worry about. Then I quit my game of Scrabble and started searching on job websites.

So it looks like it's all over for me and either Cathy or Imran. Two new people are joining and they aren't buying any new desks. I can't really complain. I've managed to ride it out for over a decade, which is pretty good going. But it's a little unfortunate for Cathy or Imran, because they both seem to work pretty hard. Unless they're just as lazy as me and really good at hiding it.

Wednesday 23rd January

I feel like I'm crossing a line with these use-by dates now. I've just eaten a ready-meal lasagne that was a whole week out of date. Rebelling against the tyrannies of your ex-partner is one thing, but this is just reckless.

I have no idea what will happen now. Maybe I'll wake up on a cloud next to Jim Morrison, John Lennon and Kurt Cobain. I'll tell them about the lasagne, and they'll greet me as one of their own – a victim of rock and roll excess who burnt out instead of fading away.

THURSDAY 24TH JANUARY

Jen asked me for the SOP on one of our accounts today. For a moment I thought I was supposed to have done some work and I'd have to dip into my bank of excuses. But then I realized she was just asking me about the state of play. So she'd managed to invent an acronym that caused unnecessary confusion, and for what? To make herself sound so busy she hasn't got time to say entire words. And how many syllables did she save exactly? None at all.

I was trying to explain this to her when her phone went off. Her ringtone is 'Mamma Mia'. Apparently, this is her favourite film of all time, and she especially likes the part where Pierce Brosnan sings.

FRIDAY 25TH JANUARY

I had a day off today. We had to use up all our holiday allowance by the end of January, so I thought I might as well book it. Given how much I hate work, you'd think I'd welcome days off, but I actually find them rather stressful.

I feel like I have to do something worthy of a day off, or I'll have wasted it. I couldn't work out if I wanted to make a start on *The Sopranos*, and while I was trying to decide I found myself watching an entire programme about car boot sales.

I tried getting round to ordering some decking for the garden, but it felt too much like work, which is definitely not right for a day off.

I then thought I should go to a museum of some sort, but this still hadn't happened by 3 p.m., so I turned on my laptop and played Scrabble. In other words, my day off was exactly the same as a day at work would have been except I had to pay for my own heat and electricity.

I really hope Josh doesn't get rid of me. I couldn't handle this much choice every day.

Saturday 26th January

This morning I got sent a brochure from Saga, a company that specializes in holidays for the elderly. At first I assumed I'd been sent it by mistake, but then I worried that I might actually be old enough to be in their target market now.

I threw it in the bin and turned on MTV Base to prove that I wasn't really old. But all the jiggling arses gave me a migraine so I turned over to a Led Zeppelin special on VH1.

All day the brochure preyed on my mind. What if they were right? What if that really is my sort of thing now?

Eventually, I dragged it out of the bin and sighed with relief as I saw it all still looked utterly horrendous. I don't want a relaxing, all-inclusive cruise with 24-hour room service and on-board entertainment. I don't want to experience distinctive cultures, traditional customs and breathtaking vistas. I don't want to be herded around tourist traps with sunburnt geriatrics spending wads of cash on tat for grandchildren who'd rather just have the money.

In other words, there's hope for me yet.

Sunday 27th January

It doesn't take much to set off my grumpiness these days. This morning I felt like I was going to sneeze, but then the feeling went away again. I spent the rest of the morning brooding about the sneeze that got away. I don't know why, I just had a feeling it was going to be a good one. Eventually, I convinced myself that other sneezes would come along and I should put it behind me.

I went to the supermarket this afternoon, and I tried to act on my resolution to be more positive by chatting to the woman at the checkout. I said that the weather was surprisingly nice for the time of year, although a colder snap was forecast. Unfortunately, I don't think she understood English very well, because she rang a bell to call out her supervisor. A scowling woman with a huge cup of coffee in her hand emerged from the back room. I didn't want to admit that I'd dragged her away from her break just to talk about the weather, so I asked if they had any charcoal briquettes. I don't know why. They were the first things that came into my head.

She dragged a 4kg bag over to the till and said it was the only size they had. I then had to lug them all the way home, even though I've got no intention of ever using them, as I hate barbecues. So this is what I get for trying to be friendly, is it?

Monday 28th January

I got the early train again this morning, as I didn't want either of the newcomers to nick my chair. In the unlikely event that I survive the redundancies, I don't want my screen facing into the office so everyone can see I'm playing Scrabble.

I noticed that Erika had placed a chair at the edge of my desk, so I made a barrier of Post-it notes to mark out my place. I haven't had to do anything that petty since I made a textbook barrier to keep out Trevor Chalkley's germs when he sat next to me in school, but I thought I'd make the effort in case I survive the cull.

Jo was the first of the new arrivals to turn up. She looked like she was in her mid-twenties, though from her dress sense you'd guess she was mid-way through primary school. She had a pink hair clip, a yellow T-shirt and a pair of black pumps like the ones we used to wear in PE before trainers became fashionable.

She was also wearing thick black glasses frames with no lenses in, which I found odd. So people who need glasses are getting expensive laser eye surgery, but people who don't need them are buying frames with no lenses in? Make your minds up, folks.

Jo said hello, took her chair at the edge of Cathy's desk, opened her thin laptop and put her white earphones in. I think she might be one of those cool people you hear about. Her little-girl image will get creepy if she sticks with it until she's my age, but right now it seems to work.

Jez turned up at half nine and plonked himself down on the chair at the end of my desk. He had ginger dreadlocks, baggy purple trousers and a waistcoat with an ethnic pattern. I remembered my vow to be less grumpy this year and tried my best not to form an instant hatred of him.

'Hi, dude,' he said, holding his hand out.

Then I recognized him. He was the little bastard who stole my chair in Starbucks. At least it meant that I could freely get on with forming my hatred of him.

Jez's wrists were covered with scraps of grubby fabric, and I asked him what they were. Apparently, he's been to eleven festivals in the last three years, and he's kept the wristbands from all of them. He went through them one by one, detailing all the macrobiotic food stalls, sustainable world music stages and costume parades he'd enjoyed. I asked him for the exact times and places of these festivals so I could be absolutely sure to never go within a twenty-mile radius of them.

TUESDAY 29TH JANUARY

Oh well, here goes. I've been invited to a meeting with Josh on Friday morning. Imran has his meeting at nine, Cathy has hers at half nine and I've got mine at ten.

Josh clearly wants to get rid of me, so why not do it right away? Then I could scrape the contents of my desk into a cardboard box and piss off without having to hear any more about Jez's gap year. He's being going on about it for ages now and he's showing no sign of stopping. Is it possible that an anecdote about a gap year could last longer than the year itself?

What is this obsession young people have with travelling, anyway? When I was young, a holiday meant sitting on a pebbly beach with your parents in the pouring rain with nothing but your seething resentment to keep you warm. Now it means playing the bongos and 'finding yourself'.

I can't help noticing that these kids who find themselves always seem to find that they like sitting on warm beaches and living off their parents' money. Must be such a revelation for them.

On my way home tonight, a woman handed me an invite to an open night at the local gym. I have no intention of ever signing up to one of those places again. Last time it took me so long to cancel my direct debit that the four trips I made must have cost about £200 each. But this was a free offer, so I thought I might as well go.

I rushed back home, stuffed my jogging trousers and T-shirt into a bag and ran out. The offer was only valid until eight, so I had to take a shortcut through the council estate. There were some frightening teenagers on bikes outside the underpass, so I had to forge an alternative route through the estate's maze of pathways.

I had to leapfrog over three randomly placed pedestrian barriers, sprint past a loose pit bull terrier and dodge several abandoned shopping trolleys to escape the estate, but I managed to get to the gym just before eight. I dashed into the changing rooms, threw my stuff on and hurried down a corridor into a bright room full of exercise machines.

A man wearing a polo shirt and tracksuit bottoms came over to me. 'Hi, I'm Jay,' he said. 'I'm here to talk you through the facilities. Do you know which ones you'd like to try first?'

I had to wait to catch my breath.

'Yeah,' I said eventually. 'Do you have a café?'

Wednesday 30th January

It's the end of January now. Time to reflect on how my resolution to be more positive is going.

Not very well, really. A little better than that year I vowed to give up drinking and then remembered about my 'beers of the world' gift pack. But overall, I wouldn't say I've managed to be positive for an entire month.

Does it matter, though? After all, if the Greeks and Romans had sat around grinning all day, would they have bothered inventing civilization? Maybe negative thinking is the driving force behind all culture. By demonizing pessimism, we're forcing ourselves into irreversible decline.

Would Isaac Newton have discovered gravity without negative thinking? Would Leonardo Da Vinci ever have drawn a woman with a wonky smile and inspired a crap airport novel without negative thinking? And would Dave Cross ever have won a bronze award for business-to-business copywriting without negative thinking?

I forgot about that award. Maybe I should bring it in tomorrow when I'm pleading with Josh. If it doesn't impress him, I could always club him to death with it.

Thursday 31st January

You know what? I don't mind being a grumpy old git. When you look at the modern world, with its coffee franchises, reality shows, banks, social networks, cyclists and funky bosses, the only rational responses are grumpiness, depression and madness. And I'm pretty sure I've chosen the best option.

I don't need pills, padded cells or art therapy workshops to get me through it all. I just settle back for a good old-fashioned rant at the idiocy of the modern world and I'm fine again.

A woman from my electricity provider called up while I was writing that last entry and asked how happy I was with their service on a scale of one to ten. I told her I was chronically dissatisfied with everything, so it would have to be a one. But I told her that as I found dissatisfaction comforting, it would also have to be a ten. She said she'd put me down as a ten and hung up. I've never had a cold caller hang up on me before. That's a new one.

FRIDAY 1ST FEBRUARY

That was weird. I came in on the early train again and watched from my desk as Imran went in for his meeting. He emerged a couple of minutes later carrying a letter, and went straight home. I think he looked sad, though it's hard to tell with him. I only found out he split up with his girlfriend when his shirts started looking more crumpled.

Cathy emerged from her meeting after just a couple of seconds, carrying a letter and wiping her eyes with her sleeve. So I knew she was a goner, unless she was crying because she'd found out she had to stay and sit next to Jez, which would be understandable.

Then it was time for my walk down the green mile. I knocked on the door and sat opposite my prepubescent executioner. Here I was, after years of hard work, about to be tossed on to the scrapheap. Well, a few months of hard work and years of skiving. But it was good skiving. I put a lot of effort into that skiving.

Josh was going on about how the company was going through a difficult time following the loss of the Donaldson Sweepers account, and how he had to restructure the team blah blah blah.

Why do they always give this preamble when they're getting rid of you? I'd prefer it if they started with insults. As I'm sure you're aware, you're a lazy bastard and we all hate you. We've put together a very generous redundancy package and we'd be very grateful if you shoved it up your arse and fucked off.

Josh had finished talking. Something was wrong. He was smiling.

'Sorry,' I said. 'Am I staying?'

'Of course,' he said. 'We've got some great opportunities coming up and we'll need someone senior around. And Steve says you've got a great attitude.'

A great attitude? Immediately, I could see what was going on. This was Steve's idea of a practical joke. Tell this little upstart I'm a good worker and let him find out the hard way that I'm as useful as a chocolate teapot.

Diary of a Grumpy Old Git

Saturday 2nd February

The shock of yesterday's non-sacking has worn off, and it's now sunk in that I've got to spend all day sitting next to a ginger Rasta who says 'dude' and 'buddy' at the end of every sentence.

There was nothing else for it. I had to go to the electrical superstore in the retail park and buy some douchebag-cancelling headphones.

As soon as I stepped into the shop, a man wearing a short-sleeved shirt pounced. I told him I was just browsing, and hurried off into the store. I've made the mistake of engaging with those people before. Listen to their hypnotic lies and you'll emerge blinking into the daylight with a trolley full of gizmos you didn't want. All of which will be guaranteed until the year 2050 because they'll have tricked you into buying warranties that were more expensive than the products.

Making my way around the maze of shelves to the headphones section at the back while avoiding the commission-hungry staff was like playing a real-life game of Pac-Man.

Finally, I reached the huge display of headphones. Why did shops have to get so big? There was a time when you'd simply wander down the high street and you'd have three choices of whatever you wanted. There'd be the cheap but rubbish one, the good but pricey one and the average one. You'd pick the average one and be home in time for *Final Score*. How are we supposed to choose between the million options we get these days?

The cheapest pair was £6.99 and the most expensive was £299.99. I grabbed the £49.99 ones and looked around for one of the men in short-sleeved shirts. Now that I actually wanted one of those little bastards, they were nowhere to be seen. Obviously.

I'm still trying to work out what happened on Friday, and I've come up with a theory. It's a little far-fetched, so you might have to bear with me. What if I'm actually pretty good at my job? I know I don't do much, but what if the small amount I do is good enough to justify my salary? Maybe I'm not a practical joke after all. Maybe Josh really will benefit from my experience. Maybe I just need to turn up a little earlier and go to a few more meetings and I'll be fine. Get me with my positive attitude. Told you I wasn't a grumpy old git.

Sunday 3rd February

I did nothing at all today. It was great. I meant to order the garden decking and watch the first disc of my *Sopranos* box set, but I just sat on my sofa drinking instant coffee and looking out the window.

It was pretty boring, but I like boredom. We're the only generation who have truly experienced it. Our parents grew up without basic labour-saving devices and they never stopped faffing through their daily list of chores. The generation beneath us are bombarded by constant entertainment options from their phones, laptops, tablets and consoles, and they've committed themselves to describing everything they ever do on their profile pages. But we're the ones who had to go to bed early because TV had stopped for the night. We're the ones who got turfed out of the pub because it was closing for the afternoon. We're the ones who spent entire mornings on the circular bus route just to pass the time.

Well, that last one might just have been me. But the point is, it's our responsibility to keep the great tradition of boredom alive and I spent today doing my bit.

Monday 4th February

Cathy and Imran didn't come in today, so I'm guessing they accepted their redundancy pay and emptied their desks over the weekend. So that's it for them. No leaving drinks, no goodbye card. Just a Stalinist removal from history. I wouldn't be surprised if smiling images of Jo and Jez had already been Photoshopped over their faces in the Christmas party pictures.

Jo and Jez moved their stuff into Cathy and Imran's desks and at lunchtime Erika handed out the new phone list. Jen, Jez, Jo and Josh were all clustered together, while I was floating up at the top of the page, a remnant of a forgotten age.

In the afternoon Josh sent us a link to a website where we have to log exactly how we've spent each working day. I can briefly remember Steve trying to introduce timesheets ten years ago. As I recall, I led a successful uprising against them with my timesheet paper plane contest. I suspect it will be harder to turn these fresh-faced idiots against the idea. Jen's already been jabbering on about what a great idea the website is.

In better news, the headphones worked. Jez started telling me about an unspoilt beach in Thailand that he visited and presumably spoilt, and I popped them on. His lips were still moving, but it was the shouty voice of Joey Ramone that was blasting into my ears.

Tuesday 5th February

It was quite frosty this morning so I made my way in carefully to avoid breaking my hip and ending up on YouTube. I almost made it all the way to work, but I slipped on a frozen puddle right outside the office window. Luckily, no one saw me, and it gave me a great idea for a game. I stood by the window with Jo and Jez and we had to predict who would slip over. You got five points if they landed on their arses, ten if they fell on to their faces, and minus ten if they made it safely across.

It was a brilliant game, the best I've invented since 'Trevor Chalkley Dodgeball' back in school. Unfortunately, Jen spoilt our fun pouring a kettle of boiling water over the icy patch. She said that an old lady could have fallen over and hurt herself. I didn't think of that. That could have been worth twenty points.

I think the game helped me to bond with my new co-workers despite Jen's party pooping. At lunch Jo even asked me what I thought of her Hello Kitty lunchbox. I said it was nice, but she said it was hideous and that's why she'd bought it. I think she's one of those ironic people. Most of her purchases are ironic, as far as I can tell. If they made irony tax-deductible she'd hardly have to pay anything.

Jo should be careful because one day she'll forget whether she's being ironic or not. I had a similar problem when I was young. I said so many sarcastic things that my voice got stuck in sarcasm mode and wouldn't go back to normal. It caused massive problems at my Uncle Roger's funeral.

Wednesday 6th February

I was sociable again today. Jo took her headphones off, so I asked what she'd been listening to. She mentioned lots of bands I'd never heard of, but I nodded in approval as if I liked them too. She might have been making them up to take the piss out of an old fogey, but I don't think so.

Jo asked me what music I liked, and I said Joy Division and The Smiths, as they were the coolest bands I could think of that I actually like. Jo nodded in approval and I sighed with relief.

Unfortunately, Jez overheard us and started wanging on about a busker he'd seen who was better than anyone with a record deal. Jo and I both whipped our headphones back on, terrified that Jez would produce an acoustic guitar from under his desk and treat us to a rendition of 'No Woman No Cry'.

I got the bus back this evening. We waited for fifteen minutes and then three came along at the same time. A woman wearing a vest and tracksuit bottoms who'd been waiting with me said, 'Always the same, isn't it?

You wait ages and then three come along at once. You'd think they'd do something about it.'

I think she was offering this as observational comedy, but it annoyed me much more than the late arrival of the buses.

'Of course three buses always come along at once,' I said. 'If the first one is even slightly delayed, more and more passengers will accumulate at each stop and its progress will be further slowed as it lets them on. Meanwhile, the buses behind will have fewer passengers to pick up and they'll catch up. The only thing they could do about it would be to make the first bus drive past without letting you on, which would make you even angrier.'

'I know,' said the woman. 'Typical, isn't it?'

Thursday 7th February

Today I wrote a list of things that annoy me about Jen. It was all I could do to keep myself sane.

1. The way she mutters as she types so we'll all realize she's working hard.

2. The way she brown-noses Josh. He mentioned he was a Chelsea fan the other day and I saw her reading their Wikipedia page right afterwards. Every time he emerges from his office to make a cup of coffee, she

follows him into the kitchen to tell him about some amazing work she's done.

3. The way she works too hard. In the cardboard box factory I used to work in, I was taken aside by one of the old duffers for a quiet word about 'making the job bad'. He said that eager newcomers always try and impress the foreman by grafting as hard as they can, but the problem is that everyone else looks bad by comparison. He told me to slow down, take as many tea breaks as I could and always take a newspaper to the toilet. It's advice I've followed ever since. Jen's 'making the job bad' for all of us now. As the resident old duffer, it's my responsibility to have a word with her about it. But what if she grasses me to Josh?

4. Her abuse of the English language. The other day Jo invited her into a meeting, but she said she couldn't go because she was 'in the zone'. Now, if I was in a very, very good mood I might just about be able to forgive a professional baseball player who used this phrase. But Jen was filling out a spreadsheet. There's no way you can be 'in the zone' while using Excel.

5. The way she glances at her phone but doesn't answer it, forcing me to relive my most harrowing cinematic experience over and over again.

Jo spotted me writing the list and asked me what I was doing. I couldn't be bothered lying, so I showed it to her.

Jo glanced over her shoulder and said, 'Thank God for that. I thought it was just me.'

It turns out everyone hates Jen. While I was bitching about her with Jo, Erika the office manager came over and joined in, as did a bloke from finance called John who I've never spoken to. Jez even joined in after a while, which surprised me. The only person I've heard him speaking negatively about before was Robert Mugabe.

We had a great time slagging Jen off. I don't know why firms spend so much money on away days. If you really want your team to bond, just wait until someone unpopular goes on holiday and then clear everyone's diaries for a session of slating them behind their back.

After about twenty minutes, Jen came back from her 'powwow' with Josh and asked what we were all laughing about, so I found a video of a sneezing kitten on YouTube and pretended we were watching that. She looked at it and said, 'That is so LOL.' I think we got away with it.

Friday 8th February

I had a blocked nose, an earache and a slight headache when I woke up this morning. I tried drinking a Lemsip, but it didn't work, so I went back to bed.

It didn't put me in a bad mood, though, as I love being ill. Not seriously ill, of course. But I've always enjoyed the sort of sickness that lets you stay in bed watching crap TV for a couple of days. Unlike the planned holiday, the sick day comes with no expectations. All it takes is a particularly tasty lozenge, an especially satisfying nap or a surprisingly informative Hitler documentary and your day is already better than you thought it would be.

The only bit I don't like is phoning in sick. I heard myself putting on a fake-sounding voice as I left a message on Josh's machine today. I was genuinely ill, but my hammy bunged-up tone made it sound like I was lying. I can only hope that, one day, civilization advances enough for us to accept that our voices don't really change much when we're ill and we can all speak normally when we call in sick.

Saturday 9th February

I felt much better this morning, which was annoying. I was hoping to drag my illness out for a few more days. Unfortunately, I had no choice but to plough through my to-do list, starting with ordering the garden decking. I selected some online and clicked the 'purchase' button. For some reason, last time I used this website I decided against storing my card details. I wonder what I was scared of. Hackers sprucing up the shrubbery?

I had to root around for my debit card and enter my details all over again, including the three-digit number that's so completely and utterly secret it's written on the back of the card. Then I clicked on 'purchase', but had to fill in all my details again because I'd neglected to type in my phone number, which was apparently a 'required field'. I clicked on 'purchase' for a third time, but this time nothing happened because my wireless connection had gone down.

I tried turning the computer off and on again, then I tried turning the router off and on again, then I tried turning my printer off and on again, just in case that was something to do with it. I looked around the flat, desperately trying to find something else to turn off and on again. Maybe the fridge was somehow involved.

There was nothing else for it. I was going to have to call a helpline. No doubt someone whose voice hadn't yet broken would sneer at me for missing something glaringly obvious, but I had no choice. I fished the manual out of a drawer and looked for the helpline number. The only thing that was given was a website address, which is very useful when your Internet access has gone down.

I typed the Web address into my phone and waited as it slowly brought up the page. There was still no number, but there was a 'contact us' link. I must have especially fat fingers, because it took me about ten attempts to click on it.

I then had to scroll through endless pages of frequently asked questions and online help request forms until I eventually found a phone number. Then I had to navigate through a confusing series of options on their automated service before I was finally allowed to speak to an actual human.

I braced myself for the condescension. But guess what? The fault was at their end, not mine. They reset the connection and it all started working again. I'd been made to feel like a grunting Luddite for wanting to use something as primitive as a telephone. And yet it was the only way I could have solved the problem.

SUNDAY 10TH FEBRUARY

I bought a magazine from the newsagent's this morning, and as I was walking home an insert about a wine company fell out into a muddy puddle. I ignored it and continued down the street, as any sane person would have done. Unfortunately, a woman with straggly brown hair darted towards me, accused me of littering and demanded that I pick it up. I explained to her that I hadn't known anything about the insert until it fell out, so I couldn't possibly be guilty. Maybe she'd like to address her complaint to the newsagent, the sales director of the magazine or the media agency who recommended that the wine company book an unbound insert rather than a full-page ad like civilized human beings. Of all the people whose decisions led to that insert floating on the puddle, I was the least responsible. Unfortunately, the woman insisted that I pick up the filthy bit of paper and fling it into a bin.

I was then forced to tramp up and down the high street looking for somewhere to wash my hands. Am I imagining this or did there used to be things called public toilets? When did they take them away? Why did no one complain? Were we all too ashamed about our bodily functions?

Well, it's too late now. If you want to urinate in public now, you have to sneak into a phone box and pretend to talk into the receiver as a suspicious trickle of liquid runs out below.

I didn't even have that option as I looked for somewhere to wash my hands. I was forced to go into a coffee shop and ask if I could use their toilets. They said they could only give out the door code if I bought something, so I had to spend three quid on a mocha just for the privilege of washing the mud off my hands. This sort of experience is the real reason that print journalism is dying. It's nothing to do with the Internet.

Monday 11th February

Josh came over to my desk this morning to check if I was feeling better. His tone was sympathetic but I could tell he was looking for evidence that I'd been skiving. I did a couple of unconvincing sniffles to help my case.

He asked how I was getting on with the time-logging website, which is worrying. I've already put a total of six hours down on it. What more does he want?

I can tell the little bastard is using that website to monitor my entire life. This is fascism! This is the thought police! It's all turning into *1984*! The novel rather than the year, that is. If everything turned into the year I watched *Police Academy* and got off with a girl who looked like Cyndi Lauper, I wouldn't be complaining.

I've ordered my decking now. I even stored my details in the website so I wouldn't have to go through all the punishment for missing out required fields again. Although it did mean that I had to sign up to the website, which was also very stressful. Above the password box it said, 'You can choose any combination of numbers and letters between six and sixteen characters long – get creative!'

What utterly shitty advice. Don't get creative. It's a password, not a Turner Prize-winning installation. Use it as an outlet for your artistic urges and you'll never get into your account again.

I used my mother's maiden name as my password, like I always do. The site told me this was 'very weak'. Thanks for that, website. I wanted you to remember my details, not evaluate my password-devising skills. Is there anything else you'd like to criticize while you're at it? Perhaps you've been spying on me through the webcam and you think my shirt doesn't go with my trousers. Jumped-up little cyber bastard.

TUESDAY 12TH FEBRUARY

Josh asked me how my workload was today. Like the snooping little Stasi officer doesn't already know. I told him it was moderate and he said he'd like me to come along to a 'chemistry meeting' with a client called TC Waste Solutions, who are apparently the second-biggest industrial bin suppliers in the south-east. Whoop bloody whoop.

He said that if we impress them, they'll give us their business, which will make up for the loss of the Donaldson Sweepers account. Then he said it was the sort of account we could 'have fun with'.

What does that even mean? How can working on something like that possibly be the same as having fun? Maybe 'fun' is one of those words that's changed its meaning now. Maybe it means the opposite of what it once did, like 'bad' and 'wicked'. It would certainly explain fun pubs.

Wednesday 13th February

I was woken up at seven this morning by the doorbell. It threw me into a panic. Was it the police? Had they finally worked out who stole that Lion bar from WHSmith in 1978? I threw myself out of bed, desperately fighting my pins and needles to drag my jeans on. I rushed to the front door, fumbled around for my key and opened it to see a deserted driveway and a card that read, 'We called to deliver a package, but you were out.' No I wasn't. It's seven in the morning, my curtains are closed and the horrified cries of a middle-aged man trying to get dressed were ringing out. Don't pretend you thought I was out.

How do these delivery men manage to leave their cards and disappear so quickly after ringing your bell? Are they somehow bending the laws of time and space? Forget the Large Hadron Collider, it's delivery men we should be studying. If we can work out how they operate we might be able to unlock the very secrets of the universe.

I glanced at Jo's screen as I was walking past her desk today, and saw she was looking at a website called Pitchfork.

I sneaked a look at the site when I got back to my desk. It turns out this is the place she gets all those obscure bands from. I followed a few links, listened to a couple of albums and before I knew it I was doing something cool again for the first time in about twenty years.

I even managed to casually drop the names of the bands to Jo later on, and she seemed impressed.

It's so easy to be cool now. In my day, you'd have to read an inky music paper, walk down to a dingy record shop, hand a tenner over to the sneering staff, carry a massive slab of vinyl home and lift it carefully on to your turntable. Now all you have to do is click your mouse and you're a hipster.

Thursday 14th February

This is embarrassing. There was a card on my chair when I got into work this morning. I was so surprised I had to go into the toilets to open it. Inside was a Hello Kitty Valentine's card which read, 'Love from ?'

No need for the question mark. It's obvious who put it there. But was Jo sending it ironically? She must have been, but I couldn't bring myself to talk about it with her. What if I told her it was a good joke, and she was actually being serious? I'd be throwing away my first genuine chance of something happening since the separation.

But she can't have been serious, can she? She must be twenty years younger than me. She probably didn't even exist on my eighteenth birthday. Not that she missed anything. I should have waited until the following Saturday for the party. I don't know why I expected anyone to turn up on a Tuesday.

Whenever Jo looked over at me for the rest of the day, I turned back to my screen. I couldn't say anything. I wasn't even good at this stuff when I was the right age for it.

I need to take my mind off all this right now. I think I'll start my *Sopranos* box set. HBO will make everything all right.

FRIDAY 15TH FEBRUARY

I've got my first meeting with TC Waste Solutions on Monday, so I spent all of today reading their website. It was so boring I had to reward myself with a game of Scrabble every time I finished a paragraph. They do everything from small pedal bins to industrial waste compactors and I had to read about the lot.

I spent quite a lot of time wondering what would make someone set up a business like this in the first place. What sort of life experience would drive you to something so boring?

On the bus home I found that I could name almost every type of bin we drove past. I need to stop filling my head with all this crap. Sooner or later I'm going to force out something important.

I'm like a pathetic teenager. A girl sends me a Valentine's Day card as an obvious joke and I spend all evening fretting about whether she was serious. Of course she wasn't serious. She's never serious about anything.

But what if she meant it? It's clearly up to me to make the next move, but what am I supposed to do? I can't get my best friend to tell her I fancy her because I'm not at school any more and I don't have a best friend. I can't wait for the DJ to play 'Careless Whisper' because we're not in nightclub and it's not the eighties. I can't even ask for her number because I sit next to her every day.

I think you're supposed to ask someone on a date these days. But there's no way I can make myself do that. Surely there's some sort of Facebook button you can click that does all that for you now.

I need to stop thinking about it and get some sleep. I've arranged the redelivery of my decking for tomorrow and I'll need to run the race of my life to reach the front door before the delivery man pisses off.

SATURDAY 16TH FEBRUARY

I was so stressed about missing the doorbell that I woke up at six and waited in the hall. I sat staring at the door like a Russian hitman, knowing that I'd have just seconds to react when the time came.

I feel asleep at noon, only to be woken up a few minutes later by the sound of the doorbell and a card being shoved through the letterbox. I jumped to my feet, threw open the door and chased the delivery van down the street. I caught it at the lights and stood in front of it, demanding that they either come back and deliver my decking or run me over and put me out of my misery.

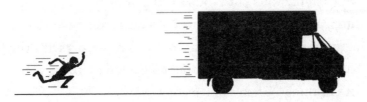

They reversed down the street, plonked the cardboard boxes in front of my door and handed over a touchscreen so battered and insensitive that I gave up on my signature and drew a picture of a house instead. It doesn't matter, because they'll never need proof that I signed for the boxes. Even if they contain nests of wasps I wouldn't go through the hassle of getting them to come back and collect them.

Now it's two in the afternoon, I've finally got my decking and it's not raining, so this would be a perfect time to start installing it. I'm far too tired to do anything of the sort, of course. But I've beaten the home delivery system, and that's the main thing.

I know I could cut out all this delivery hassle if I got a car again. Sarah took the car when she left. I meant to buy another one but I found that getting by without one improved my quality of life considerably.

Having to spend a day on stakeout to catch the delivery man is annoying, but compared to having a car, it's nothing. When you've got a car...

Actually, I don't want to get started on cars. It's getting late now and if I open that old wound again, I'll be scribbling about cyclists until this diary is full and the morning light is peeping through the curtains.

SUNDAY 17TH FEBRUARY

I popped out to the cashpoint this afternoon, and I couldn't believe my luck when I saw there were no dotty geriatrics queuing for it. The machine wasn't out of order and the screen wasn't even smeared with kebab grease. It was my lucky day.

Then something really strange happened. I forgot my PIN. I've had the same PIN for almost a decade. I must have used it thousands of times. Yet today I tried to remember it and I couldn't. It wasn't like I knew it would come back if I waited or hit myself hard enough. It had gone. I'd dragged it into trash, emptied the trash and dropped the laptop into the bath.

It was because of that sodding bin website, wasn't it? I knew I'd dislodge something important.

So now I could tell you that the thing on the wall next to the cashpoint was a two-litre galvanized steel cigarette bin. But I had no idea what the four digits that would allow me to function as a normal member of society were. I just wish my brain had deleted something I didn't want to remember, like the last five years of my marriage.

I ejected my card and saw that a queue of angry people had formed behind me as I'd faffed around. It turns out there was a dotty geriatric at the cashpoint today after all. It was me.

MONDAY 18TH FEBRUARY

The TC Waste Solutions office was in an industrial estate full of mini roundabouts and signs about fly tipping. The meeting room looked out on a yard of large metal bins. Cigarette smoke drifted across from the workers huddled in the porch, adding to the grim, post-apocalyptic feel. The biscuits were pretty good though. I reckoned I could get through the meeting if I focused on them.

The head of the company came in and started telling us about his bins. I tried my best to take notes, but there was something about him that was distracting me. Why did I feel like I should be flicking him on the ear and throwing his briefcase out of the window?

I stared up at the bald, overweight man sitting opposite me in disbelief. TC Waste Solutions? The initials were right. But that couldn't be it. I couldn't really be sitting opposite Trevor Chalkley, could I?

I looked down at my notes and covered my face with my hand. I'm pretty sure I got away with it. He probably doesn't remember the people he went to school with anyway. Who does?

Tuesday 19th February

I sent Jo a Facebook friend request today and she accepted it. Seems like a good sign. I'm pretty sure that's how it all starts these days.

It's such a strange way of doing things, though. In my day, if you'd asked a girl for a list of events she was attending in the near future and a copy of all her photo albums, she'd have hit you with a restraining order. These days it's the norm.

Before I sent the request I thought I'd better check through the stuff I've 'liked', in case any of it was too middle-aged. I clicked 'unlike' on gardening, hiking and Bruce Springsteen.

Sorry, Boss. I'll make it up to you by listening to *Darkness on the Edge of Town* tonight.

WEDNESDAY 20TH FEBRUARY

I was looking through Jo's Facebook photos at lunchtime when I noticed that she'd uploaded one of herself in a bikini. She was pulling a funny face and pointing to her sunburn, so it was obviously intended to be ironic. But it was nonetheless a picture of her without many clothes on.

I wasn't sure if it would be acceptable for me to look at it, but I couldn't resist. Then I thought someone might peer round at my screen, so I tried to make it go small again, and I accidentally clicked 'like'.

I gibbered at my screen in panic. Jo had uploaded over a thousand pictures and I'd 'liked' the only one of her wearing a bikini. My heart sped up as I realized what a lonely, creepy stalker this made me look like. Then it went even faster as I realized how much of a lonely, creepy stalker I actually was.

As soon as I calmed down, I spotted an 'unlike' option, so I clicked it and all the evidence of my crime seemed to disappear. Jo returned from the sandwich shop a few minutes later, and looked at the screen as she munched her feta and olive wrap. She didn't spew it all over her laptop, so I'm guessing I got away with it. But I think I'll stay off Facebook for the time being.

THURSDAY 21ST FEBRUARY

Josh was hovering around my desk this morning when I skulked in. He said that he had brilliant news for me. Apparently, Trevor Chalkley thought the chemistry meeting had gone well, and he'd decided to give us the account.

'Impressed much?' shouted Jen from the other side of the room. Then she started applauding, and everyone else joined in. I'm sure she was just doing this to crawl to Josh, but it still felt quite good. It had been so long since I've had anything resembling success at work I'd forgotten what it was like.

I thought Josh was about to shake hands with me but he held his palm in the air instead. I stared at his hand in horror as I realized he wanted me to high-five him. I gritted my teeth and did it. Jen whooped. As soon as everyone got back to their work, I went to the toilets to wash my hands. But no matter how hard I scrubbed, I couldn't erase the shame of the high-five.

I went to the supermarket on the way home to stock up on ready-meals. When I told the woman behind the counter that I needed plastic bags, she gave me such a scowl that I opted to buy yet another organic Fairtrade 'bag for life'. I must have about twenty of those things now. I want to get rid of some, but 'bag for life' sounds too much like a threat. I expect some sort of carbon-neutral hit squad will come round and finish me off if I attempt to bin one of them.

No time to think about all that now. I'm off to bed early tonight. I need to be at TC Waste Solutions at nine tomorrow for my briefing. I feel like I ought to do a decent job after all that applause.

FRIDAY 22ND FEBRUARY

When I got to TC Waste Solutions this morning, the receptionist showed me into Trevor's office. I was hoping there might be a few people in the meeting, but it was just the two of us. I shook his hand as quickly as I could and looked down at my notebook, hoping he wouldn't recognize me.

Trevor launched straight into one of his monologues about bins, and I thought I was safe. Unfortunately, he stopped after just a couple of minutes.

'You think I've forgotten, don't you?' he asked.

'Forgotten what?' I asked.

'You're Dave Cross from Oakland Comprehensive School. You invented that whole "Chalky Balls" thing.'

I hadn't realized I was the one who'd come up with it. I felt an odd surge of pride.

I looked up at Trevor and tried to sound surprised. 'Jesus, is that you, Trevor? It's been so long. How are you doing, mate?'

'We weren't mates,' said Trevor. 'You made that clear at every single opportunity. Don't think that I've forgotten that barrier of books you used to build if I ever sat next to you. So you wouldn't catch Trevor germs.'

Trevor pointed to a framed picture of him standing next to a bin. 'I bet you wish you had caught Trevor germs now. Then maybe you'd have your own business rather than working for someone who wasn't even born when we were at school.'

He dragged a photo of a plump woman wearing too much eyeliner out of his wallet. 'Look at my lovely wife.' He followed it with a picture of two glum girls. 'Look at my children. This one has been predicted straight As in her GCSEs and this one has Grade 8 in the cello. Has your daughter got Grade 8?'

'I don't have a daughter,' I said. 'Can we get on with the meeting now, please?'

'Don't tell me what to do,' he said. 'From now on, you obey me. And if you question anything at all I'm going to fire your shitty little agency and blame it all on you. Do you understand?'

'Fine,' I said. 'Whatever.'

Trevor pulled a packet of chalk out of his bag. He took out one of the pieces and crushed it with his stapler.

He pointed at the pile of chalk dust. 'Rub that on the front of your trousers.'

'Oh, come on,' I said.

'I'm serious,' said Trevor. 'I'm calling your boss if you don't do that in ten seconds. Ten … nine … eight …'

I scooped up a handful of chalk and rubbed it across the front of my jeans.

'Happy?' I asked.

'It's a start,' he said. 'It's a start, Chalky Balls.'

SATURDAY 23RD FEBRUARY

I think it was a mistake to go down the high street this afternoon. I find it stressful enough at the best of times, so attempting to get down it after yesterday's meeting was asking for trouble.

Pavements are just as important as roads. Why don't pedestrians have to pass tests and get licences? And why can't we punish people who use pavements incorrectly? I encountered a few I'd have banned for life today.

First I was stuck behind a woman who was texting as she walked. Does this multitasking really save any time? Can't she just wait at the side of the pavement, text her friend and then continue at a normal walking pace? Or is she unable to stop texting at any time?

Next I got trapped behind a young couple walking hand in hand. And there was a pedestrian barrier at the side of the pavement so I couldn't even overtake them. I'm guessing that the barrier was there to prevent accidents. Well, it nearly caused one today. It would have caused a couple of fatalities if I'd had an assault rifle.

Finally, my path was blocked by a woman with a pram who'd stopped to talk to her friend, and had for some reason chosen to park it across the entire width of the pavement. Now, I'm all in favour of people having children and sustaining the human race. Actually, no I'm not. I don't have to be in favour of it if I don't want to be. Let's all stop procreating and let the grey squirrels take over the planet. You can tell they've got their eyes on it.

So all in all, it wasn't a good day for a woman in a fluorescent tabard to leap into my path and ask if I wanted to help some donkeys. I told her that I didn't give a fuck about donkeys. They don't have to use banks, wait for trains or worry that their phones are out of date. And, more to the point, if she gave a fuck about donkeys, she'd be down the stables tending to them rather than getting an hourly wage to bully direct debit details out of vulnerable pedestrians.

There was a boy at our school called Alex who used to block your path in the corridor and charge you 10p to get past (50p if you were Trevor). We all thought he was acting weirdly because he came from a broken home. Little did we know he was simply ahead of his time.

SUNDAY 24TH FEBRUARY

I'm definitely going to lay the decking in the garden today. Decking will make everything better. Decking will fill the void.

Update: I didn't get round to laying the decking. I spent this morning writing a letter to the council about how they should divide the pavements into fast and slow lanes, so people who want to mill around and chat can keep to the left and people who actually want to go somewhere can stick to the right.

In the afternoon I called Brad on his mobile and pretended to be a property developer. I told him I was interested in buying the most expensive house he had, but I was only in town for a day, so I needed to see it this afternoon. You could tell he was weighing up the inconvenience of working on a Sunday against the possibility of a big fat bonus. His greed got the better of him and he arranged to meet me outside the property at five.

I wanted to go and watch him slapping his dashboard in frustration as he realized no one was coming. But then I worried that he might bring Sarah along, she'd point me out, and he'd come over and beat me to death with his BlackBerry. So I stayed at home and imagined him getting angry instead.

I'm not sure why I feel the need to annoy Brad like this. He took Sarah off my hands. I should be thanking him. But there's something about those dead eyes I saw on Facebook that makes me want to keep picking on him. Even Sarah isn't punishment enough.

Monday 25th February

I was woken up by a car alarm at six this morning. It clearly didn't wake up the owner of the car because they didn't come out and switch it off. How are those things supposed to prevent theft? The only thing the alarm announced was that no one who gave a shit about the car was within earshot, so you might as well go ahead and nick it. I was considering breaking in myself, just so I could drive it into a canal.

I seem to live my life against a constant backdrop of alarms now. My new microwave beeps every minute until I take the food out. Heaven forbid that I should leave my carbonara inside until it's cool enough to eat. The only effect these arrogant little gadgets have is to make us block out all alarms, so we ignore the important ones like the smoke alarm in the orphanage. Thanks, microwave. Hope you're happy with yourself.

Amazingly, things got even worse when I dragged myself out of bed and attempted to eat some corn flakes, as I'd run out of granulated sugar and had to use caster sugar instead. Why do I buy caster sugar? Do I ever find myself overwhelmed by the urge to bake fairy cakes? No, I just use it as a disgusting substitute when I run out of proper sugar. You might think that a simple solution would be to buy two packets of granulated sugar next time, instead of one of each kind. But I know I won't. I can guarantee I'll have exactly the same problem again in three months' time.

With two major annoyances before 7 a.m., I decided to write the day off and go into work early. I was so tired I couldn't even enjoy Scrabble, so I made a start on the brochure instead. But here's the weird thing. I kept going until I finished it. I didn't even stop for lunch. I don't know what came over me. Maybe I've caught workaholism from Jen.

Tuesday 26th February

Jen was behind me in the sandwich queue this lunchtime, so I felt like I should make conversation. I tried complaining about queuing, but she said she didn't mind it. I tried complaining about the sandwiches, but she said she liked them. How are you supposed to make small talk with someone who won't moan? I even resorted to complaining about the local area, assuming that no one could find anything positive to say about that. But Jen said she liked it because it had a 'village-y vibe'.

No it doesn't. It's right in the middle of a city. It couldn't be less like a village. And why would we want it to be? What's so great about places where everyone has six fingers and no passport? Why spend all your money moving to a city and then obsessively seek out the bits that aren't like one?

Jen waited until she got to the front before reading out the options on the blackboard. Then she chose something, changed her mind, changed her mind again and asked if the hummus was organic. A man in the queue behind us tutted, and a woman looked at me and shook her head. I don't see what it had to do with me. I chose my order before I even got in the queue. I had the exact change ready and everything.

WEDNESDAY 27TH FEBRUARY

Josh popped over this morning to check how I was getting on with the brochure. According to my diary, he wasn't supposed to see it until Friday. How did he know I'd had a fit of madness and finished it? Maybe I was typing too loudly.

I printed out the document and showed it to him. He skimmed through and said, 'This is really punchy.' It made me feel really punchy when he said that. And really slappy. And really stabby.

'We should fire this off now,' he said. 'Get ahead of ourselves.'

Fan-fucking-tastic. So now I've got to find something else to pretend to do for the rest of the week in case he comes over for any more impromptu meetings.

THURSDAY 28TH FEBRUARY

My hair's getting out of control again. If I look at it from the front it's just about neat enough. But if I turn my head even slightly to the side I transform into a maths lecturer who's been dragged through a hedge backwards.

I need to go to the barber's, but I can't face it. I'd honestly rather go to the dentist during an anaesthetic

TIM COLLINS

shortage. Last time I tried to get my hair cut, I didn't get any further than the moody black and white shots of male models in the window. Why are those preening himbos supposed to entice us in? And why do they always look so deep in concentration? Are they trying to count higher than ten?

If I were a barber, I'd have no photos at all in the window. Just a sign that says, 'We'll give you exactly the same hairstyle as you've got now, only a couple of inches shorter, and you won't have to describe what you want in any way. We won't even ask where you're going on holiday this year.'

I suppose I should be grateful. Most men my age find themselves pulling clumps out of their bath plugholes as their hairlines retreat backwards. But at least they don't have to go to the barber's.

No news on the brochure front yet. I keep expecting Trevor to call me into an emergency meeting where he'll steal my lunch money and give me a wedgie, but I haven't heard anything at all. Maybe he's had his little revenge now, and I'll never have to see him again.

FRIDAY 1ST MARCH

I snotted out my latte in surprise this morning. Even though she was sitting just a few feet away from me, Jo emailed to ask if I wanted to come for a drink. I said I'd be glad to, and asked what the secrecy was for. I was hoping she'd say she wanted some time alone with me, but no such luck. She was simply inviting everyone by email because she didn't want Jen to come.

I looked over at Jen, who was flicking through a woman's magazine and repeating the words 'That is so true' to herself. I told Jo I thought it was a good idea.

I have to admit I was getting my hopes up that everyone else would leave early, and I could finally ask Jo about the Valentine's Day card.

Then just before five, my phone went off. Like an idiot, I answered it.

'Hi, it's Trevor. I've just got a few comments on the brochure copy.'

'Great,' I said. 'Can I give you a call back?'

'No,' he said. 'You can't give me call back, Chalky Balls. Remember what I said? Do what I say, or the account's walking and several tons of shit are going to fall on your head. Now, my first change is to page one, paragraph one, sentence one, word one…'

114

Jo was getting her bag ready. I put my hand over the receiver and said, 'I'll see you down there.'

Jen's head popped up from her desk. 'Oh, are we going out for a drink? Cool bananas.'

Jo tutted and shook her head.

'Sorry,' I whispered.

I eventually finished the call at quarter past ten. Trevor had carefully gone through every word and explained why it was wrong and also why every other word would also be wrong. Then he told me he expected to see a revised version first thing on Monday.

Everyone had gone from the pub by the time I'd arrived there, but it didn't matter. It's not like I could have got drunk anyway. I've got to be up at seven tomorrow to work on the brochure.

SATURDAY 2ND MARCH

The Great Escape is on TV today. There's a sale at the local garden centre. And an old friend is in town and wants to know if I can meet up for a pint. But none of this is relevant to me because I've got to write this stupid brochure all weekend. Is this how it's going to be now? Seven-day weeks with early mornings and late nights? Perhaps I should stop dividing time into weeks at all and get on with the mind-numbing, soul-destroying work that will fill all my time between now and death.

SUNDAY 3RD MARCH

Even sleep isn't a respite any more. I had a dream about bins last night. It wasn't even an interesting one. I was just walking through a yard full of bins and ticking a clipboard. I wonder if Josh will let me put the dream down on the time-logging website.

I thought it was Monday when I woke up. Then I realized it was actually Sunday and for a couple of brief seconds my spirits lifted. But then I remembered it was a Sunday I'd have to spend working and my spirits plunged right back down again.

Today was obviously determined to be utterly horrendous, so I admitted defeat right away and got on with the brochure. At lunchtime I cooked macaroni cheese and watched the shopping channel, as I knew that if I tried to do anything remotely pleasant, today would find a way to ruin it for me.

Monday 4th March

I sent my brochure copy to Trevor this morning. A minute later I got a reply which read, 'This is great. Thanks.' Another minute later I got an email which read, 'Actually, this is all wrong. I'll arrange a meeting soon to discuss.'

At least this is helping me get over my guilt about how we treated Trevor in school. All my life I've had this niggling sense of regret about the time we dipped his Kit Kat in the urinal. Now I wish I'd dipped his face in it.

Jez saw that I was scowling and asked what the problem was. I didn't want to go into the whole Trevor thing so I pretended I'd accidentally deleted a file.

'Take a chill pill, buddy,' he said. 'It's not that big of a deal. See the bigger picture.'

Why are all the phrases about calming down so fundamentally annoying that they have the opposite effect? If Satan exists, I have no doubt that he spends his time concocting them. 'Could you keep an eye on the lake of fire for me? I'm off to combine the words "chill" and "relax".'

Tuesday 5th March

I completed my coffee shop loyalty card this morning. Finally getting the tenth stamp made me feel like I'd really achieved something. But then I felt so revolted with myself that I ripped the card up and threw it in the bin. Is this what counts as achievement now? Never mind defeating fascism or putting a man on the moon. I got £33 worth of coffee for just £30. Big deal.

I've had it with loyalty cards now. I'm not touching one again. With that dangerous distraction out the way, I'm sure my true purpose in life will become clear.

Jez mentioned something about Jo's party today. This was the first I'd heard about it. I wanted to ask Jo about it, but I thought it would be embarrassing if I wasn't invited. And why should I be? She wants to hang out with people her own age. She doesn't want an ancient git like me skulking in the corner and reminding everyone of their mortality.

I can't believe I'm fretting over whether I've been invited to a party or not. Whenever Sarah said we had to go to one, I used to pretend I had a headache so I could stay in and watch TV. She'd even sometimes trick me into going by asking how I felt before revealing that we were off to some horrendous social gathering or other.

Well, now I can stay in and watch all the TV I want, and I find myself wanting to go out and speak to people. This would infuriate Sarah if she knew. I'll be sure to mention it if I ever see her again.

Wednesday 6th March

It turns out I was invited to Jo's party after all. The invitation was sent on Facebook, which I hadn't checked for a couple of days. I had a momentary stab of delight when I discovered this, but this was soon swamped by my usual self-loathing. I couldn't believe I was happy because someone had invited me to their party. Am I fifteen years old? Gee, it looks like I will go to the prom after all. Pathetic.

I accepted the invitation and went out to get my hair cut right away so I wouldn't have time to dread it. I was about to pretend I had a doctor's appointment when I realized there was no point. If you come back to work with shorter hair, it's pretty obvious where you've been. Anyway, if Josh gets on my case I'll tell him that I worked through the weekend.

There was no queue in the barber's on a Wednesday afternoon, so I plonked myself straight down in the chair, asked for a little off the back and sides and gritted my teeth. Whenever I get my hair done, I'm convinced that it looks so weird that strangers in the street will point and laugh, and then no one notices at all.

That's pretty much what happened today, except that someone did notice. Jo noticed. That's a good sign, right?

THURSDAY 7TH MARCH

I tried to save a Word document today, but my laptop said there wasn't enough memory. I turned it on and off again, deleted as much as I could from the hard drive and updated the operating system, but nothing worked. It looked as though I was going to take it to Graham the IT guy.

I usually search online for help with computer problems, as I hate asking IT guys for help. It's one of those things like going to bed before eleven or buying slacks that makes me feel like I'm crossing a line into old age. I used to see Steve calling Graham into his office to ask him how to underline words and attach files to emails, and I swore I'd never degenerate into such technological senility.

But today I had no choice. There was something wrong with my computer, and it surely wasn't too much to ask the person we employ full time to look after them to help.

I was worried Graham might see how long I'd spent googling Scrabble hints, so I deleted my history before walking down the corridor to his foul-smelling room. There was a poster on the door that read, 'Keep Calm and Turn it Off and On Again'. I knocked, and braced myself to be patronized.

Graham was playing a game where he had to shoot terrorists in an airport. He paused it, and I handed him the laptop.

He bashed the keys, using shortcuts instead of dropdown menus.

'I see you've deleted your history, you dirty old sod,' he said.

'Yeah,' I said. 'I was ashamed of how long I've been spending on Scrabble websites.'

'Course you were,' said Graham. He did a crude wanking mime and said, 'Ooh, I got a triple word score.'

I smiled in a shameful effort to stay on the right side of him until he'd fixed the laptop.

After a few more minutes of clattering around, Graham said, 'The hard drive's screwed' and handed me a new laptop.

I walked back to my desk in astonishment. Could it be possible there was someone even lazier than me in the office? And that all you have to do to survive as an IT guy is adopt a sarcastic tone that scares everyone off and then dish out a new computer if they ever go to see you? I'm in the wrong line of work.

Not that I'm complaining. This new computer runs Scrabble about four times faster.

I started fretting about my wardrobe today. The only clothes I own are the white shirts and black jeans I wear to work, and the blue jeans I wear as a treat on weekends. I wondered if something more exciting might be required for a party, so I stopped off at one of those clothes shops that plays loud music.

As soon as I stepped into the shop, a man wearing a baseball cap at a strange angle asked me if I was looking for anything in particular. I told him I was just browsing, but he insisted on following me round and saying, 'That would look really good on you, I've got one just like it at home' every time I went near something. At least those electrical store guys piss off when you tell them to.

I found myself buying a red hooded top with Japanese writing on it just to shut him up. I don't even know what the Japanese characters mean, but I'm guessing they translate as 'gullible twat'.

I tried on the hoodie when I got home and I looked like the dwarf from *Don't Look Now*. Then I stuck it

Tim Collins

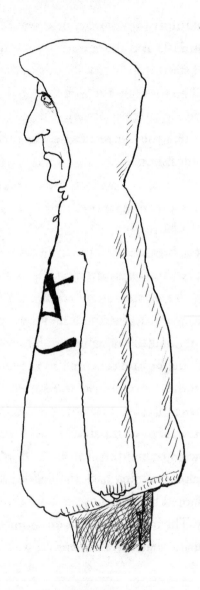

in the back of my wardrobe, next to the skinny jeans I bought in 2003 and the trainers I bought in 1998. I'm thinking of starting a charity shop with that stuff. All the profits will go to 'Help the Middle Aged', a foundation that will raise awareness of vain, deluded, mid-life crisis men who think they have any business whatsoever in a trendy clothes shop.

FRIDAY 8TH MARCH

I went out at lunchtime to try and find a suitably ironic birthday present for Jo. At first I went to a shop that sold things like *Ghostbusters* T-shirts and *A-Team* pencil cases. I was about to buy her a Hello Kitty purse when I realized that all that stuff was deliberately ironic, so it wouldn't be impressive enough. I wonder if all those children in the Third World who work eighteen-hour shifts to make this stuff know it exists only to be sneered at by emotionally constipated hipsters with no capacity for genuine enjoyment?

I was making my way back to the office when I noticed a charity shop. I held my nose and went inside. I found it right away. The irony mother lode. A porcelain Princess Diana figurine that plays a wonky electronic version of

'Candle in the Wind'. It was the most horrendous thing I've seen in my life. I knew Jo was going to love it.

Saturday 9th March

I know this sounds unsettlingly positive, but I'm really looking forward to the party tonight. I honestly can't remember how long it's been since I went to a proper party. I wonder if you're still supposed to turn up with a vinyl copy of *Dare* by The Human League and a tin of Twiglets?

I suffered through more than my share of dinner parties and barbecues when I was with Sarah, of course. But this isn't the same thing. It's a proper party where you turn up with a bag full of cheap lager rather than a fancy cheesecake. And you roll a spliff and talk about the cosmos rather than sip a cheeky Beaujolais and talk about house prices.

Speaking of which, I really hope they aren't expecting me to bring any drugs. I don't think I'd be very good at buying them. I've still got a few antibiotics left in the bathroom cabinet. Maybe I'll bring those.

Sunday 10th March

How can I be hungover? I wasn't even remotely drunk last night. I know I turned up with twelve cans of lager, but they disappeared as soon as I put them in the fridge. I can't have had more than four in total. Is that all it takes for a hangover now? If I'm going to put up with this throbbing headache I at least want a few hours of release from crippling self-awareness.

On the positive side, Jo loved the Princess Diana statue. She asked me where I got it, and I told her I saw it advertised in the *Daily Express* and paid in monthly instalments. Then she gave me a hug and peck on the cheek. Thank you, Princess of Hearts!

On the negative side, I did feel a little too old to be there. All right then, a lot too old. I didn't really know anyone, but it didn't matter because the music was so loud I couldn't hear what anyone was saying anyway. I tried to strike up a conversation with some of Jo's friends but all they did was nod and look around the room for someone more interesting to talk to. After a while I started saying things like 'I've killed and I'll do it again unless someone stops me' and I got the same response.

Jo's friends soon abandoned me by the snack table so I tried every mathematically possible combination of crisps, vegetable shavings, nachos, salsa and sour cream to make myself look busy. After a while, Jez took pity on me and came over to chat. He soon brought the topic round to his gap year, but I didn't mind. I was actually grateful to hear about his spiritual awakening in the Far East. That's how bad things were.

An hour later 'Hey Ya!' by OutKast came on and everyone started dancing so I turned my attention back to the dips. I hate dancing. I didn't mind it when I was younger, but things were different then. Nobody could dance. These days they teach them how to grind to hip hop in infant school. If I tried to so much as nod my head in time with the beat everyone in the room would have vomited and the party would have been abandoned.

Jo saw me on my own and tried to drag me into the middle of the room. I shook my head and let go of her hand. Five minutes later I went home. When I'm in a nursing home in a few years' time, I'll probably look back on that as the moment I threw away my last chance of happiness.

MONDAY 11TH MARCH

Jo thanked me for coming to her party when I got in this morning. She didn't seem angry about my refusal to dance, if she remembered it at all. Jez said he was sorry he didn't make any sense, but he'd just smoked a massive joint when he spoke to me. I felt like telling him he was exactly the same as usual and his dealer is clearly selling him Oxo cubes.

Jen looked up from her screen and narrowed her eyes whenever anyone mentioned the party, so maybe it was worth going after all. That's right, Jen. I'm in the cool gang and you're not. Get over it.

Also, I was tagged in a few Facebook photos that made me look like I was actually enjoying myself. I hope Sarah sees them. She was always going on about how I didn't know how to enjoy myself. Well, here's the proof, Sarah. All it took was the removal of a particular person from my life for the party to start.

TUESDAY 12TH MARCH

Trevor has invited me to another meeting tomorrow. I got the email first thing this morning and I spent all day worrying about it. It didn't help that Jez had a really annoying sniffle that I couldn't force myself to complain about.

I could feel myself getting tenser with every sniff, but I didn't say anything. If you complain to sniffers, you look neurotic and they get to feel like they're doing you a massive favour by blowing their noses rather than letting the same bit of snot travel up and down their nasal passage all day.

Sniffers are like terrorists. If you let them know they've got to you, they've won. You just have to ignore them and get on with your life. And dispatch a unit of Navy SEALs to assassinate them when they drop their guard.

Wednesday 13th March

Trevor kept me waiting for half an hour this morning before calling me into his office. He kept his eyes fixed on his computer screen, so I took a chair and waited for him to speak.

'Morning,' I said after a while.

Trevor held his hand up to silence me.

After a couple of minutes I asked, 'So, where are we at on the brochure?'

'Did someone speak?' asked Trevor. 'I thought I heard someone speak.'

I had a vague memory of saying this to Trevor on the school coach once.

'Come on,' I said. 'This is getting boring.'

Trevor turned away from his computer at last. 'You should have thought of that before you bullied me, shouldn't you?'

'I didn't bully you,' I said. 'I just sided with the bullies so they wouldn't pick on me. And gave them the odd suggestion every now and then. It's not the same thing. Can't you let it go?'

'I don't need to let it go,' said Trevor, digging his fingernails into his palms. 'It was the best thing that ever happened to me.'

Trevor took a plate out of his desk drawer. 'Biscuit?'

Rather than the usual array of bourbons and digestives, the plate contained nothing but an unwrapped Kit Kat in a pool of yellow liquid.

'No thanks,' I said.

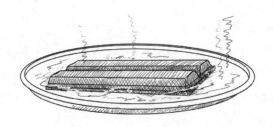

Trevor shoved the plate closer to me and an acidic smell drifted up into my nostrils.

'Eat the biscuit,' said Trevor.

'I'm not hungry,' I said.

'Neither was I,' said Trevor.

I tried to remember the day we dipped Trevor's Kit Kat in the urinal. I'm pretty sure we didn't make him eat it.

'Eat it,' said Trevor. 'Or I'll call Josh and tell him you've screwed up. That I'm resigning the account and telling all your other clients to do the same unless your company puts you out to pasture.'

I looked at the Kit Kat. OK, so it had been pissed on. But would it kill me? Would it even make me ill? Didn't people in lifeboats sometimes drink urine to survive?

I lifted the Kit Kat slowly towards my mouth.

Trevor let out a squeal of laughter and clapped his palms together. 'Oh my God. You were actually going to do that, weren't you?'

THURSDAY 14TH MARCH

I think Trevor has stopped now. As soon as he'd done his Kit Kat prank yesterday, he switched back into serious mode and went through the brochure like a normal, sane adult. I made a few changes to it this morning, sent it over, and he approved them right away.

Josh came over to my desk to congratulate me, and I sank back in my chair so I wouldn't have to high-five him again.

'Well done for getting that off the desk so quickly,' he said. 'I thought Trevor was going to be a much trickier customer.'

It's very simple, Josh. Clients are pushovers as long as you're prepared to eat chocolate wafers they've marinated in their urine. That's the first lesson of business.

I was still thinking about Trevor on my way home when a GE Business Catering van drove past. It had 'We bring a lot to the table' written on the side of it. That was my slogan. That was the campaign I won my bronze award for.

I should have been proud that a line I wrote ten years ago was still in use. It should have restored my confidence after the Kit Kat incident. But realizing that my biggest professional achievement amounted to nothing more than a few words on the side of a van delivering soggy sandwiches to bored businessmen only made things worse. When I think back to the early promise I showed when I invented the nickname 'Chalky Balls', it's nothing short of tragic.

FRIDAY 15TH MARCH

A new action movie opened today starring Vin Diesel, The Rock and Nicolas Cage. Jo said it sounded like the worst film of all time, and before I realized what I was doing, I suggested we should go and see it. She agreed, and I'm meeting her outside the multiplex in the retail park at seven tomorrow.

I'm not entirely sure, but I think that counts as a date. I was tempted to refer to it as such to see if it made her throw up in her mouth, but I didn't want to risk it.

We didn't really do 'dates' last time I was single. As far as I remember, we used to go down to the local bar and drink ourselves senseless in the hope that we'd wake up with Miss World. It wasn't a very reliable system, but it was better than all those speed dates and compatibility questionnaires you have to bother with now. Trying to get a shag these days is like applying for a fixed-rate business loan.

Saturday 16th March

I've spent all day getting ready for my date tonight. I've showered, brushed my teeth, sifted around in the bathroom cabinet, found some Old Spice, dabbed it on, realized I smelled like 1979, showered again, put on my only pair of genuine Calvin Klein pants, worried that if Jo somehow ended up seeing these she'd realize I had high expectations, replaced them with my Primark pants, ironed my jeans, thought they looked too neat, found a different pair, put my vest on, took it off again, put my shirt on, buttoned it all the way to the top, thought this looked too formal, undid the top three buttons, thought this looked too sleazy, did one of them up and brushed my teeth again.

Now I'm worrying that Jo is going to turn up with loads of friends and say, 'You didn't think it was a date, did you? You're such a hilarious old codger.'

I'd forgotten about all this crap. It's almost as bad as sitting on the sofa with Sarah watching home makeover shows and dying inside. Almost.

SUNDAY 17TH MARCH

Jo met me in queue and gave me a quick hug. She wasn't wearing her fake glasses, and I wondered if this was because of our date, but it was actually because we all had to wear huge 3D glasses.

It was the first time in about ten years that I'd been to one of those kinds of cinemas. Sometimes I'd go and watch something miserable and subtitled with Sarah, but it's been a while since I've seen the kind of film where beefy male models rob banks. It featured lots of shots of them walking away from explosions without flinching. As someone who soils their trousers whenever a car backfires, I found this rather difficult to believe.

It was quite hard to hear the dialogue above the noise of idiots grazing on popcorn and answering their phones, but I don't think anyone minded. Two hours of loud noises and bright colours would have kept that lot happy. Any shape they could recognize as a person or a car was a bonus.

I kept my glasses on when I went to the toilet halfway through, to see if they'd make real life look more 3D, but they just made me slip on some popcorn.

After the film we went to a theme restaurant in the retail park. I'm not sure what the theme was, but I think it was the futility of existence. Every few minutes the waiters would run up to a table carrying sparklers and start singing 'Happy Birthday'. It was quite apt because I felt like just being there aged me by several years. I think it was one of those 'fun' places.

Jo said the film was the worst thing she'd ever seen and I agreed with her. Then she said it was also the best thing she'd ever seen and I agreed with her again. For some reason, the bill came to more than it would have done in a good restaurant, but I paid it anyway.

Then we left and got into the cab rank. I knew this was the bit where I was supposed to make a move, but it had been so long I'd forgotten what to do. Was I supposed to ask her if we could kiss or just angle my head to the side and open my mouth? I was just about to try the latter when I remembered about the onion rings on my burger. If I blasted her with onion breath, she'd be going home in an ambulance rather than a cab. I decided I'd hold off until next time.

Yeah. Like there's going to be a next time.

MONDAY 18TH MARCH
Josh invited us all to something he called a 'kickstart' meeting this morning. Every time he said 'kickstart', he did an inverted quotes mime with his fingers, as if the

meeting wasn't really called this at all. It was basically a pep talk about how we should all work harder and make him more money. Jen whooped at the end of every sentence and I wanted to start kicking her. Maybe that's where the name comes from.

Josh announced that we were pitching for the business of a forklift truck manufacturer in Manchester on Friday morning. I immediately started to think of excuses why I couldn't work on it, but then he thanked Jo for agreeing to do the presentation.

I thought about this for a second. That meant Jo would be staying over on Thursday night, and so would I if I worked on the pitch. I suddenly remembered that I'm incredibly interested in forklift trucks and I've always wanted to find out more about them.

Josh was overjoyed when I volunteered to work on the pitch and said he was glad that his 'kickstart' meetings were already having an effect. And yes, he did the finger quotes again.

Tuesday 19th March

I'd better get something out of all this, because working on the forklift account is unbearably dull, and I had to stay until ten tonight. I asked Josh if he wanted me to get on with the Web copy, but he said there was no point until we'd cracked the 'big idea'. I asked why we didn't just show pictures of warehouse workers standing next to the machines and explaining how they rely on them. Josh said I wasn't 'pushing the envelope' enough and went back into his office. Then at quarter to eight he emerged holding a picture of a worker standing next to a forklift. 'This is it,' he said. 'This is the idea.'

So that's what 'pushing the envelope' means. Making someone wait around all day and then passing off their ideas as your own. Finally, at eight o'clock, I made a start on the Web copy at a time when I should have been making a start on my lasagne ready-meal.

WEDNESDAY 20TH MARCH

This is just great. Josh was worried that Jo had too much work on, so he's taken her off the pitch and put Jen on instead. So now my reward for all this unpaid overtime is an overdose of Jen's blathering. Maybe I should tell Josh that I've just remembered that I'm not remotely interested in forklifts.

It's ten o'clock and I'm still at work. I was just packing my things away at five to six when Josh came over with something he referred to as a 'shopping list'. This was basically a load of things I had to do before the pitch tomorrow. Except that he didn't say I had to do them, he said I had to 'action' them. It seems that the verb 'do' wasn't good enough for people like Josh, so they had to invent a premium business-class version with extra legroom and a complimentary glass of champagne.

Josh put his coat on after he'd handed me the list and it became clear that he intended to action absolutely fuck all himself. I was annoyed at first, but then I realized he'd given the same list to Jen. And I can tell from her muttering that she's almost got through it. As long as I keep perfectly still I reckon she'll finish the list before she realizes I'm supposed to be working on it too.

Thursday 21st March
I shared a cab down to the station with Jen this afternoon. We might have been on time if she hadn't stopped off at Josh's office to tell him how 'stoked' she was.

We didn't have time to queue for the only open ticket window so we had to use one of the machines. I typed in the destination, and it displayed about twenty different ticket options. We selected the most expensive one and made a run for the train.

We dashed on board with just a few seconds to spare, only for the conductor to tell us that the train would be departing twenty minutes late. Thanks for telling us before we did the 200-metre suitcase hurdle.

Most of the seats were taken, but there were a couple of singles left. I tried to hide my delight that I'd be sitting on my own for the journey rather than listening to Jen go on about the pitch.

I sat down, popped my headphones on and settled back for a relaxing couple of hours of music. The first song had hardly started when Jen came over and asked the man next to me if he'd mind moving so we could sit together. He said he wouldn't mind at all. Of course he wouldn't.

I found that Jen didn't leave any gaps in her conversation for me to reply, so I didn't have to concentrate on what she was saying.

While she was wittering on, I heard the teenager opposite complaining to the conductor that the wi-fi was too slow. I felt like shaking the ungrateful little bastard by the shoulders.

I remember being amazed the first time I saw a digital watch. No more working out the time from the big hand and the little hand. Now we could read numbers from a display.

I remember being astounded the first time I saw a Sony Walkman. No longer would we have to choose between listening to *The Dark Side of the Moon* and walking down to Woolworths. Now we could do both at once.

And I was overjoyed when I got my first cash card. No more fretting over how much money we'd need for the week ahead, now we could take it out as we pleased. We could even withdraw money on a Sunday. Imagine that.

And now this little shit was hurtling through the countryside at over a hundred miles an hour with all the information and culture he could ever consume at his fingertips, and he had the nerve to complain it wasn't fast enough.

Maybe things will be better when society collapses and we return to a medieval bartering system. As we gather on desolate hillsides to tell tales of magic glowing rectangles and huge metal birds in the sky, we'll finally appreciate what we had, and understand what spoilt little children we were.

Friday 22nd March

I know times are hard, but you'd think we could have afforded a better hotel than the one we were booked into. As soon as the receptionist handed me an actual metal key rather than a plastic card, I knew I was in trouble.

Smoking was apparently prohibited in the hotel, but that didn't stop my whole room, from the threadbare carpets to the yellow curtains, smelling like it had been coughed up in a bronchitis ward. The window rattled in its frame whenever there was a slight breeze, and managed to keep me awake in the short gap between when the couple in the room above stopped shagging and when the kids in the room next door started shouting.

There was a sign above the towels asking me to reuse them to avoid the unnecessary use of detergents. Judging by the brown stains on the back of them, the necessary use of detergents has also been avoided. How utterly committed to saving the planet this establishment must be. I can't say I noticed their solar panels or recycling bins, though. It's funny how they're most committed to the environmental initiatives that save them effort.

Breakfast was included in the price, but not in my definition of 'edible'. To make things worse, it was presented as if it were normal food. The instant coffee was served in a small metal pot, the cheap own-brand cereal was stored in a plastic tube with a 'Kellogg's Corn Flakes' logo stuck on, and some thin, tasteless red liquid had been syphoned into a tomato sauce bottle.

The pitch seemed to go pretty well, though. I know Jen's relentless positivity can be annoying, but it was very handy in the meeting. She did a terrific job of coming across like she was actually excited by their range of forklifts. Maybe she actually was excited by them. Maybe she's excited by everything all the time. I have no idea.

We sat together on the train home, and once again I didn't need to add anything to the conversation to keep it going. She asked me what I thought about new government plans for a high-speed rail link and then argued alternatively for and against them all the way home. It sounds crazy, and it was. But I found it strangely comforting. In fact, her chattering lulled me off to sleep after about twenty minutes. She might have stopped talking at that point, but I seriously doubt it.

SATURDAY 23RD MARCH

On my way down to the shops this morning I pressed the button on the pedestrian crossing and the 'WAIT' sign lit up. While I was standing there, an old lady came along and pressed the button again. I couldn't believe it. It was like she had so little faith in my ability to press a button she felt she had to do it again to make sure. I tried to explain this to her and she said I was being rude.

I pointed out that she was clearly the rude one. If you see someone waiting at the lights, the very least you can do is credit them with the intelligence to press a button correctly. Unfortunately, it took me so long to explain this to her that we both missed the lights, and the button needed to be pressed again. I offered to let her do it this time, but she refused in case I shouted again. Which proved she hadn't been listening to a word I'd been saying.

As I approached my house I noticed that a woman had very thoughtfully stopped right outside to let her pit bull terrier shit in my driveway. I glared at her, but she just smiled and said it was a nice day. There was no attempt to apologize or scoop up the faeces. Both lady and dog just stood there grinning at me.

I was about to tell her that I made no distinction whatsoever between someone who lets their pet defecate on my driveway and someone who hitches up their skirt, drags their knickers down to their knees and curls one out herself. Unfortunately, I didn't get the chance because the horrible dog jumped up at me.

I flinched back.

'Don't worry,' said the woman. 'It just means he likes you.'

So shitting on someone's driveway and trying to bite them is a way of showing approval now, is it? My grasp of etiquette is clearly out of date.

SUNDAY 24TH MARCH

I bought a Sunday paper from the supermarket while I was out this morning, and when the woman behind the counter asked if I wanted a bag, I declined. I know how angry they get about plastic bags and I couldn't face buying another bag for life, so I decided to tuck my paper under my arm. Unfortunately, I then stopped off on impulse at the corner shop to buy a chocolate bar, and the owner accused me of stealing the paper. I tried to explain that I'd already bought it from the supermarket, but he asked why it wasn't in a bag. I couldn't really be bothered arguing with him, so I paid for it again.

I felt obliged to read every section of the paper after paying for it twice, when all I'd really wanted was the crossword and the TV guide. So I lost half my morning and most of my change as a result of trying to help the environment.

I hope the environment realizes I'm expecting the favour to be returned soon. It could start by striking the corner shop with lightning.

I just had an enjoyable evening of going through my spam emails. Every time I click on 'spam' to see if an actual email has ended up there by mistake, I'm confronted with a bizarre menu of mankind's unspoken longings. It appears we'd all like larger wangs and a bucket of Viagra so we could 'experience pleasure like never before'. Then we'd like to buy genuine Rolex watches at knockdown prices and gamble the money we've saved in online casinos. We'd like to look younger, lose weight and be awarded fully recognized degrees based on our current knowledge and life experience. Then we'd like long-lost relatives, Nigerian princes and heads of Chinese banks to transfer millions of dollars into our bank accounts.

Someone somewhere is clicking on this stuff. There are people out there thinking, 'You say you want to give me some free money, eh? Tell me more.' And these people have bank accounts.

If I were a billionaire I'd pretend to be a Nigerian prince and email random people to ask for their bank details. If anyone ever gave me them, I'd transfer a million quid into their account right away. It would make one gullible idiot very happy and everyone else in the world feel like they'd spent their lives discarding genuine opportunities for wealth.

MONDAY 25TH MARCH

We won the pitch! Hooray! That means I'll have to do more work. Boo. I must try and make our presentations crapper in future. I want the company to win enough business to keep going, but not so much that I have to stay until nine every night.

Josh took us all to the pub for champagne after work. I didn't get much of a chance to talk to Jo, as she was sitting down the other end of the table, while I was stuck talking about the pitch with Jen and Josh.

I didn't say much because I knew my voice would take on a sarcastic tone just to spite me, and I didn't want to upset Josh and Jen. I don't really know why. They were drinking champagne and braying at the tops of their voices. I should have been annoyed, but they were so excited about winning the business I actually felt pleased for them. I must be going soft.

Jo left after a couple of hours and I said I'd walk her to the tube. We passed the Red Lion and I asked her if she fancied something to eat. I must have been feeling courageous after all that champagne.

I was expecting bar snacks, but it seems that the Red Lion has been turned into a gastro pub. The silent old men with their pints of stout have been replaced by smart couples drinking wine, the pork scratchings have been replaced by vegetable shavings and the 'ladies' and 'gents' signs have been replaced by ambiguous squiggles designed to confuse everyone into wetting themselves.

The waiter showed us to a candlelit table and handed out menus with words like 'confit', 'infused' and 'jus' on them. I suddenly realized that we were having an actual, proper date in a posh restaurant. This was it. I'd been gifted another chance after screwing everything up last week.

And it's a chance I would have done something about if one of Jo's friends from university hadn't spotted us.

'I don't think we've met,' she said, extending her hand. 'You must be Jo's dad.'

And that was it. The chance had gone.

TUESDAY 26TH MARCH

I'm convinced it's all over now. If there was a remote possibility of anything happening with Jo, last night will have snuffed it out. She can hardly parade a coffin-dodger like me to all her friends. I need to move on and buy a Harley-Davidson or grow a ponytail or whatever else you're supposed to do when you have your mid-life crisis.

Today Josh told me that Trevor wants me to go in on Monday for an emergency briefing. He said he knew that Monday was a bank holiday, but the TC Waste Solutions account was important, so we'd better play ball.

I'm sure Trevor thinks he's getting another of his little revenges by dragging me in on a bank holiday. But the joke's on him, because I hate bank holidays. I'd rather spend the day in his grim office than watching half a Bond movie and failing to lay the decking.

I discovered I didn't have any food in the house when I got home so I had to call a pizza. I only wanted a small one, but the man said the minimum amount I could spend was ten pounds, so I had to get a medium. Then he said it was only two pounds more to get a large so I might as well get that instead. Then he said it was only a pound more to get garlic bread, potato wedges and a Coke so I might as well get that.

When the delivery boy finally managed to find my flat, he spent so long counting out my change in five-pence pieces that I told him not to bother. I sat down on the sofa, fifteen quid poorer and clutching enough lukewarm food to make Jabba the Hutt undo the top button of his jeans. At least it explains all those oddly shaped people you see waddling around town. They phone up for a pizza, get conned into ordering enough to feed an entire African village and before they know it they're wearing a smock and driving a mobility scooter.

WEDNESDAY 27TH MARCH

I've just been mugged. Sort of.

I was planning to eat my pizza leftovers tonight, but at the last minute I decided I couldn't face it, so I took a shortcut to the supermarket through the council estate.

As I was passing the adventure playground, a child wearing a matching blue tracksuit and baseball cap asked for 50p to call his mum. I told him that public phone boxes didn't work any more and that if I gave him 50p he'd only spend it on crisps and glue. The little bastard started snivelling, and said his mum had forgotten to come and fetch him. I don't know why I was taken in by this performance. I just didn't think he was old enough to be a criminal. Sometimes even my levels of cynicism and mistrust aren't high enough for modern life.

Anyway, I was duped and I told him he could use my phone to call his mum. Needless to say, as soon as the little thief's paws were on the phone, he scarpered off through the playground and into the estate.

I know I should go to the police, but I'm too ashamed to tell them I was mugged by a ten-year-old. I considered calling them anyway and pretending someone much older had stolen it. But what if they caught someone matching my false description and they got sent to prison? I don't think I could live with that on my conscience.

It's not losing the phone that's really pissed me off, though. Graham from IT is in charge of our work phones, so now I'll have to beg him for a new one.

THURSDAY 28TH MARCH

Graham's office was even smellier than usual this morning. Takeaway boxes were stacked everywhere, and one of the piles collapsed on to my leg, spilling rancid sweet and sour sauce into my turn-up.

'I'm assuming you enabled remote wiping?' Graham said.

'Er ... I'm not sure,' I replied.

'I'll take that as a "no". But you'll surely have kept a note of the IMEI?' he asked.

'Just remind me…'

Graham sighed. 'The IMEI, or International Mobile Equipment Identity, is a unique fifteen-digit number that anyone with modicum of intelligence makes a note of when they get a new phone. In the unlikely event that someone is too brain-dead to activate remote wiping, it's used to disable stolen phones.'

'I think I might have forgotten,' I said.

'Of course you did,' said Graham. 'Looks like we'll just have to proceed using your serial number, which was…'

I shrugged.

Graham shook his head and yanked open the bottom drawer of his filing cabinet. 'You've proved yourself incapable of looking after modern technology, so I'm going to make the punishment fit the crime.'

He held up an old-fashioned phone with a keypad. 'This is the Nokia C1-01. It has no touchscreen. It has no Web access. There are no apps on it. Want to access your email on the go? It's very simple – you can't. In short, it's a phone that no self-respecting person would be seen dead with. And as of now, it's your phone.'

I thanked Graham for his understanding and help and thrust the shameful handset deep into my pocket.

It was reasonably sunny at lunchtime, so everyone from our office complex squashed into the tiny square of grass outside. I'm not sure why I joined them. Summer is one of those things I assume is going to be more pleasant than it actually is. Maybe it's because the weathermen always say we'll be 'basking' in sunshine.

Or perhaps it's because I wear exactly the same clothes all year round, so I spend most of the summer carrying my jacket over my arm, with dark patches spreading from my armpits. I just can't bring myself to wear a T-shirt and shorts. Who knows what it might lead to? I might 'chillax'. And then I'd have to kill myself.

I was just about to give up my space on the grass when Jen came over to join me, so I had to stay out for the rest of lunch. She lay down to soak up the feeble rays and started going on about how 'fab' the sun was. I told her the sun was a big fiery bastard that made my TV harder to see and I couldn't wait for it to stop bothering me and implode. Jen laughed and called me 'Grumpy Bear'.

Grumpy Bear? He was one of the Care Bears, wasn't he? Even relentless negativity reminds Jen of fluffy teddies. It must be horrendous to be her.

At five, everyone went down to the pub to celebrate the start of the Easter break. Jo asked me if I was coming, but I said I needed to get home. I couldn't tell, but I think she might have been slightly disappointed.

So is that it? Have I stopped making a fool of myself now? I'm surprised. I'd have put money on it ending in humiliation. At least it means she can go and find herself a nice little boyfriend her own age and nobody will ever mistake me for her dad/granddad/Yoda ever again.

FRIDAY 29TH MARCH

Believe it or not, I managed to have some fun on my day off. I was glancing at Facebook this afternoon when an old work acquaintance called Dan posted: 'Just had a lovely shit.' I tried to remember if Dan was the sort of person who liked to describe their bowel movements in great detail. I was pretty sure he wasn't. A couple of minutes later, the post disappeared and another one went up, which read, 'Sorry about that. Fraped.'

I guessed that 'fraped' means someone hacked into his account. This gave me an idea. I clicked on to Brad's page and scrolled through his details for password clues.

Then I remembered. Sarah had an infallible password system, which involved rearranging your address and date of birth. I was sure she'd have imposed this system on Brad and I was right. I worked out his password and I was in.

This was it. I was a genuine hacker, like those spotty teenagers who get arrested for breaking into the Pentagon computers.

Bradley Sanderson
Confession time: Who else eats paper? I can't be the only one, can I?

Someone called 'Sandra Barker' liked that. Strange girl.

I dialled it up a notch:

Bradley Sanderson
Nobody really gets out of the bath to piss, do they? Tell the truth...

168

No responses to that one. Even Sandra Barker wasn't that weird. Next I tried:

Bradley Sanderson
Just stuck a pube in the office coffee jar. Who will win the pube lottery? It could be you.

Again, there was no response. I wondered if I'd made my fraping too obvious too soon. I deleted the posts and tried a different tack:

Bradley Sanderson changed his relationship status to **single**.

The first response said, 'Sorry to hear that. What happened?' The second said, 'Hope U R OK.' I hit the jackpot with the third response, though. It read, 'To be honest, mate, I think you were spared.' I 'liked' this comment and logged out.

Saturday 30th March

My bathroom tap stopped working today, so I had to call out a plumber. I did a Google search and chose the one nearest to my house. He said he was too busy to come, but miraculously managed to find the time when I offered him an extra twenty quid.

He turned up at 8 p.m. and I showed him to the bathroom. I always find it stressful when tradesmen come round because you're supposed to call them 'mate' but I find it too embarrassing.

'What's the problem, mate?' asked the plumber. He was chewing gum with his mouth open, which was putting me on edge. I just wanted to point the problem out and leave him to do his plumbing.

'There's no water coming out of the tap,' I said. I tried to force out the word 'mate' but for some reason I said 'dude' instead. I think I must have caught it from Jez.

The builder looked at me in confusion before crouching down and inspecting the tap. He unscrewed a small bit of metal from the end and held it up.

'Blocked aerator,' he said. He scraped some dirt out of it with his finger and screwed it back on. The water came out in full flow again. I waited for him to say something about how it wasn't a proper plumbing job

170

so I didn't have to pay, but he just looked at me and chewed his gum.

I winced and handed over the cash, including the painful extra twenty. He stuffed the money into his pocket and made his way down the driveway.

'Thanks,' I shouted after him.

'Anytime,' he said, getting into his van. 'Party on, dude.'

I tried watching TV tonight. There was a reality show about some stupid people shouting at each other. There was a programme where some celebrities from the eighties were quite rightly tortured for wanting to be famous again. Then there was one of those talent contests judged by talentless idiots who think it's possible to have a million per cent of something. At least, I think it was a talent contest. The only thing they seemed to be showcasing was their recent personal misfortune. Maybe they've cut the performances from these things now and they're just competing over who has the best sob story.

The picture quality on all this stuff was brilliant, of course. I got so excited when high-definition TV came out that I forgot there's nothing worth watching any more.

You'll be able to see all the action in pin-sharp detail, they said. But they forgot to tell us that the action we'd be able to see in pin-sharp detail was a former boyband member eating a kangaroo's testicle. You'll believe they're actually in the room with you, they said. But they forgot to tell us that the person we'd think was in the room with us was a woman spewing into the gutter outside a nightclub.

Thanks a lot, HD. Where were you when man walked on the moon? Where were you when Frost interviewed

172

Nixon? Where were you when Debbie Harry was on *Top of the Pops*? It's all well and good being around now, but don't you think it's a tad late?

SUNDAY 31ST MARCH

Today is Easter Sunday, which means we're supposed to eat overpriced chocolate to celebrate Jesus coming back to life. I can't quite remember the link, but I think it's something to do with rabbits. I'm pretty sure they explained it at school.

I spent the day unscrewing the ends from all my taps. How can something so simple have caused me so much inconvenience? Why had no one ever told me to do that if a tap stops working? You'd think the guy who put them in might have mentioned it. To be fair, he probably would have done if I hadn't been hiding so I didn't have to call him 'mate'.

This new phone isn't quite the punishment Graham said it would be. I think I actually prefer it. You don't have to click on any minuscule icons before making a call. You just press the numbers and then the call button. The camera's so terrible I never consider getting it out, which means that if I see something interesting like a sunset or motorway pile-up, I can enjoy it without worrying about taking a photo. And best of all, I can't get emails on it, so I get a proper break from work when I'm away from my computer.

It's possible that onlookers would point and jeer if I used it on the street, but I hate phoning in public anyway. I've had so many train journeys ruined by idiots yelling into their phones that I try not to inflict that pain on others. But if I ever had to use it in public, at least I'd know nobody would want to nick it. And that's a feature Apple will never be able to build into their phones.

MONDAY 1ST APRIL

None of the lights were on in the TC Waste Solutions offices when I arrived, but the door was open.

I made my way through reception and down the murky corridor to Trevor's office. I wondered if he would be waiting behind one of the filing cabinets, ready to spring out and force a pissy chocolate bar down my throat.

I found Trevor inside his office, inspecting a grey box file.

'So what was this urgent project?' I asked.

'There isn't one!' he shouted. 'April fool!'

I shrugged. I'd forgotten it was April Fools' Day, but I certainly didn't mind getting out of another tedious brochure.

'That wasn't one of the great April fool jokes, was it?' I asked.

Trevor lifted an ancient Letts diary out of the box file and flipped through the dusty pages.

'Let me see,' he said. 'April 1st. "Dave Cross told me that Mandy Riley would give me a blowjob if I gave her a pound and said the password 'Hubba Bubba'. Mandy slapped me and told Mrs Mitchell. Now I have a week of detention." Was that one of the greats?'

'It wasn't bad,' I said.

Trevor took a diary with flaky yellow pages out of the box. 'April 1st. "It turns out that today wasn't a no-uniform day after all. It was just another prank by Dave Cross. I was sent home by Mr Jenkins, but not before

Dave had rubbed chalk on the crotch of my birthday jeans." Was that one of the greats?'

'Again, it was a decent effort,' I said.

The next diary that Trevor pulled out of the box was so old that the front cover had fallen off. 'April 1st. "Dave Cross told me that a bird had done a shit on the back of my blazer. When I took it off to look he grabbed it and threw it in one of the large bins. I had to climb in to get it and when I did Dave got everyone to spin the bin round and round." Was that one of the greats?'

'OK,' I said. 'That one was a bit mean. I'm sorry.'

'Well, don't be,' said Trevor. 'While I was lying in that bin, watching the grey clouds spin round and round, I made a vow to do something with my life. And now I own the second-biggest industrial bin supplier in the south-east. Do you have your own business?'

'No,' I said. 'You know I don't.'

'That's right,' said Trevor. 'Because I'm a winner and you're a loser. Now for the real April fool joke. I do want you to write me another brochure, after all. I want it to cover our full range of galvanized wheel bins and I want it by close of play tomorrow.'

177

Tuesday 2nd April

Three hours. That's how much sleep I had because of that shitty brochure. I went to sleep at four, and had to set my alarm for seven to have any chance of finishing the thing.

I couldn't even make myself a coffee this morning because my kettle broke. I tied it in a plastic bag, chucked it in my wheelie bin and ordered a new one. I felt a slight twinge of guilt over this. I'm sure there was a time when, if something broke, you'd take it back to the shop and ask them to mend it.

178

But where would I have taken that broken kettle? Did I pay for a guarantee when I bought it? Did I fill out the little warranty form in the box? Did I even keep the receipt? Would the men in short-sleeved shirts in the electrical megastore look at me like I was bonkers if I showed them a broken kettle? I'll never know because new ones were only £20 on Amazon. And even if I'd had enough sleep the humiliation of begging for help in that aircraft hangar wouldn't be worth £20. But at least I felt mildly guilty while chucking it in the bin. That's something.

I was in the office even before Jen, and I got on with the brochure as soon as I sat down. I was hoping to take some time out for lunch, but my computer rudely interrupted me just before eleven to tell me it wanted to update its operating system. I foolishly clicked 'accept' and as a result I spent my only break of the day staring at a progress bar and willing it to speed up.

My laptop obviously sensed weakness because it kept telling me I had to install 'critical' updates for all my other programmes. I clicked 'Accept' on everything and agreed to the endless lists of terms and conditions. I had absolutely no idea what I was agreeing to, and I doubt anyone does. We'll probably just be woken up one night by armed soldiers with Apple logos on their uniforms, demanding that we hand over our first-born children as detailed in the iTunes small print.

At a quarter to five, I send the brochure copy through to Trevor and slumped forward on to my desk. While I was drifting off to sleep, Jez invited me to his party on Saturday. I was so tired I told him I didn't want to go, which was surprisingly mature of me.

I'm right, I shouldn't go. The only reason I'd want to go would be to make another pathetic attempt with Jo. And now I've accepted that will never happen, I don't have to waste a night shouting over the top of dance music in some sweaty council flat. I can settle back in bed with a mug of cocoa and a Jane Austen novel and wait for the sweet release of death, just as someone my age should.

Wednesday 3rd April

I had to go to a presentation about new media in a hotel in town today. It was unbelievably dull but I kept myself awake by imagining how I'd kill Trevor if I had an unlimited amount of time and a full Black & Decker toolbox.

Jen came along too and she spent every coffee break introducing herself to people and commenting on what a great networking opportunity it was. You're not supposed to admit you're networking. That's like admitting you're chatting them up.

She kept bringing people over to meet me, which I suppose was nice of her. I could always call them and beg them for work if Trevor gets me fired.

Jen gave me a lift home in her Land Rover afterwards, which was also nice of her.

'Leave the car at home?' she asked. I was so used to her sentences ending with an upswing that it took me a while to realize she was asking a question.

'Oh, I er … don't have a car.'

'Really?' asked Jen. 'I thought you'd be one of those car men. Is it an environmental thing? I know this one's a bit naughty, but it's fab for hills.'

'Nope,' I said. 'I wouldn't drive a car if they invented one that farted out rainforests.'

'So why don't you have one?' she asked.

'It's just … Don't get me started on cars.'

'Go on,' said Jen.

'Well, it's the speed cameras and the fines and the congestion charges and the sleeping policemen and the "Baby on Board" stickers and the pigeon shit on your windscreen and the pedestrians who veer out into the road without taking their eyes off their phones and the difficulty of maintaining a speed that's slow enough so you won't get a fine but fast enough that you don't end up annoying everyone else and getting stuck behind caravans on bank holidays and Sunday afternoons in Halfords and conversations with distant relatives about whether A roads are quicker than motorways and traffic wardens fining you for being a millimetre over the white lines and the garages that say they'll have your car ready by Tuesday and then pretend they have to send off for some parts because they didn't get it done on time and men with squeegees who throw filthy water over your windscreen and demand money to wash it off and people who sneak into the parking space you've been waiting half an hour for and getting a puncture on a motorway at night and trying to work out how to use the jack so you won't have to make a humiliating call to the AA and getting stuck with an ambulance behind you and a guy who doesn't seem in much of a hurry in front and not knowing what the button next to the steering wheel does and pressing it only for nothing to happen and drivers who've somehow passed their tests without learning how to signal and drinking mineral water because you're the designated driver at a party that would need at least three bottles of gin to get through and BMW drivers who can afford to pay the fine so they double park and stick their hazard lights on while they pop into Waitrose for some sun-blushed tomatoes...'

'OK, I get it, grumpy bear,' said Jen.

'But I haven't got on to cyclists yet,' I said. 'They're the part I hate most.'

Thursday 4th April

Another of Josh's 'kickstart' meetings this morning and this time the finger quotes went into overdrive. Apparently our latest account wins show we're 'on the runway' and we've got the 'bandwidth' to succeed. If he doesn't stop using these buzzwords soon, he'll give himself repetitive strain injury. He said he'd like more of us to 'take ownership' of accounts to foster an environment of 'co-opertition'.

Josh used the phrase 'what I like to call' so much that he even started saying it before perfectly normal words

184

like 'results'. When he's at home he probably asks his wife for 'what I like to call a cup of coffee with what I like to call two sugars'.

I drifted off about ten minutes into Josh's bullshit, but I'm sure I heard him mention the word 'hotdesking' at one point. I think that means everyone has to move desks all the time for no reason other than to introduce the stress of musical chairs into the workplace. If he thinks I'm going to give up my spot against the back wall just so he can trot out more jargon, he can shove it up his bandwidth.

This afternoon I told Jo I wasn't going to the party, and I think she was upset. Actually, I have no idea if she was upset or not. She never gives anything away. But what if she was? What if she's going through the exact same thing as me? What if she's writing a secret diary about her feelings for an older man in her office? After all, she was the one who started it with that Valentine's card. It was probably ironic, but what if she really meant it?

I tried to take my mind off things by watching a film tonight. I browsed through all the film channels I subscribe to, and at first it looked like good news. There was *Arthur*, *Get Carter*, *Straw Dogs* and *The Wicker Man*. All movies I wouldn't mind seeing again. Unfortunately, they all turned out to be appalling remakes. Who exactly are these remakes for? Do modern filmgoers find they can't follow the plot if the actors have outmoded clothing and hairstyles? They have no problem believing that costume-wearing vigilantes can defeat criminal gangs with their homemade utility belts, but show them a pair of flares or an unruly sideburn and you've lost them.

Friday 5th April

Josh came over this morning to tell me that Trevor thinks I'm doing a great job on the brochures. He said this was a terrific example of someone taking ownership of an account, and he was glad someone had been listening to his talk about co-opertition.

On the surface, it seems strange that Trevor should flit between threats and praise, but I think it's just another childish bullying tactic. If you punch someone in the arm every time you pass them in the school corridor, they learn to expect it and it stops having an effect. But if you randomly alternate between punching and friendly greeting, it's much worse. It's the hope that you might not get hit or your brochure copy might not get rejected that really gets to you.

Jez reminded me about the party before he left today. I told him I'd changed my mind and that I wanted to go. I was looking at Jo today as she fumbled her pretend glasses around. Then she looked over at me and I turned back to my screen. I'm sick of all this. I've got to ask her if she's interested. And Jez's party could be my last opportunity for a while.

Yes, it will probably end badly. Yes, it will make everything at work awkward. But I've got to do it. Life

187

is not a rehearsal. Though if it is, I'll be sure not to start watching *Lost* again in the hope that it leads up to a satisfying conclusion.

Saturday 6th April

I've just bought eighteen cans of lager, a crate of red wine and a bottle of vodka. Now it won't matter how much gets nicked, I'll still be able to get trollied.

I've just had a thought. What if I make a start on all this booze now?

The only times I've ever managed to get anywhere with women have been when I'm plastered. So what if I start tucking in to all this now? I'll probably wake up in Jo's bed tomorrow morning with a huge smile on my face.

Is that a good plan?

Probably not. But it's worth a try. I'll start with the vodka.

Sunday 7th April

It's one in the afternoon and I still have absolutely no idea what I did last night. I think something terrible happened, but I don't know what.

I've got to go now. It's going to be difficult for me to write between the bouts of vomiting.

I had a flashback while I was throwing up. I was dancing to 'London Calling' by The Clash. I think I'd chosen the track, and everyone was dancing too. They were having a great time. Maybe I actually had a good night. Maybe nothing terrible happened after all. Excuse me a minute.

Another spew, another flashback. This one wasn't so good. I was talking to Jo. It was much later in the night, and I was clutching a half-empty bottle of vodka. Sorry, I mean a half-full bottle of vodka. Must try to be positive at times like this. I'm not sure how well I was explaining myself, but she didn't look pleased.

Oh Jesus Christ. I made a move on her. I actually tried to snog her. I lunged forward, turning my head and opening my mouth. Imagine the vodka reek that must have been leaking out. No wonder she pushed me away. At least I've remembered what the terrible thing was.

I think I'm going to be sick again, but why? I've already barfed up everything from last night. Maybe I agreed to store somebody else's food in there for them.

That one was just stomach bile. Soon I'll only have this thumping headache and crushing humiliation to cope with. I had another horrible memory while I was chucking all that up. I was sitting on a sofa and watching Jo snogging a man of her own age. I think I was crying for some reason. Jez was sitting next to me, and forcing me to drink a pint of Coke. So *that* was the terrible thing.

I'm just dry heaving now. Can someone tell my stomach that there's nothing else to come out? Perhaps it would like to stop telling me to rush to the bathroom to mime throwing up. This is a hangover, not a drama workshop.

The last flashback I had was really strange. It was much later in the night and I think…

I think I was snogging Jen. *Jen!*

Did that really happen? Did she even go to the party? Or am I remembering an alcohol-fuelled dream?

Another flashback came with that last heave. I was staggering away from Jez's house. I must have been so drunk I forgot that cabs exist. And that I live in the opposite direction.

Oh. That's why I was going the wrong way. And that's what the terrible thing really was. I was heading back to my old house. The house where I lived with Sarah for ten years. The house where she still lives.

Another flashback. I'm ringing the doorbell. Stop it, brain. Don't show me this. I don't care what I did. I just don't want to know.

Brad is answering the door. I'm ranting at him. I think I'm confessing about the spam, the fraping and the prank call. Sarah is coming to the door and pushing him away. She's talking to me in soft voice, saying she understands how hard things have been for me, and that they've been hard for her too. She doesn't seem angry at all. Until I projectile vomit through my fingers and it splashes all over her dressing gown. Then she gets angry. So *that* was the terrible thing.

For some reason my mind is telling me that I still haven't remembered the terrible thing yet. But what could be worse than what I've already remembered? I haven't lost a limb. My teeth are all still there. And I'm pretty sure I didn't rip my scrotal sack open on a barbed-wire fence. So what could it be?

Ah. *That* was the terrible thing. When I finally arrived at home I sat down in front of my laptop instead of going to bed. Thankfully, I didn't manage to remember my Facebook password. But I did get into my email. I know because I saw the following in my 'sent items' folder:

To: Trevor Chalkley
From: Dave Cross
Subject: YOU ARE A TWAT

WHAT I SAID YOU ARE A TWAT MATE. SO WHAT IF IM DRINK I DON'T CARE. I HATED YOU THEN AND I HATE YOI NOW CHALKY BALLS DICKHEAD. AHHH.

OK. I've finally managed to get the childproof lid off the Anadin, and I can think straight again. A lot of terrible things happened last night. There will probably be some embarrassing consequences. But they will only be embarrassing if I let them be. It's not too late to revive my New Year resolution to be positive about everything. Trying to deal with this in any other way would result in mental breakdown.

MONDAY 8TH APRIL

When I got in this morning I dashed down to Graham's office and asked him if it was possible to delete emails you've already sent.

'It's perfectly simple,' he said. 'You just need to travel back in time and hit yourself on the head with a frying pan before you click "send". But make sure you don't speak to yourself, or you'll create a quantum paradox and doom the universe.'

I forced out a high, squeaky laugh as if I were enjoying the way the pedantic little loner was milking his rare moment of superiority.

After that I sat down at my desk and said hello to everyone as if I had nothing to be ashamed of. Jo ignored me, Jen smiled awkwardly and Jez patted me on the back and call me a 'legend'. Quite a few people giggled when they saw me today. Even Josh asked if I was 'always that shade of red'.

OK, so maybe I blushed a little. But I'm still going to look on the bright side, just as I resolved to do. I'm still alive. No one killed me. And as far as I know, I didn't kill anyone. That's something.

I was watching the news tonight and there was a feature about binge drinking. It was shot in the town centre on Saturday night, and it showed a group of girls shrieking and showing their bras to the camera. I noticed a familiar figure moving through the back of the shot, and I peered at the screen.

It was me. I was staggering down the street with my hands planted firmly in my pockets. Yet I had no memory of being anywhere near the town centre on Saturday.

The report cut to an interview with a paramedic who was complaining about the strain all these drunks were putting on his resources. There I was again, ambling around in the background with my hands in my pockets, hitting a lamppost with my shoulder.

Finally, the reporter delivered a piece to camera. Once again I staggered past, only this time I was going the opposite way. Was this some sort of editing trick? Or had I really been walking aimlessly back and forth?

OK, I need to look on the bright side again. No one has called or texted me since the piece was broadcast. No one has posted it to YouTube or tagged me on Facebook. So I can safely assume that no one else saw it.

TUESDAY 9TH APRIL

Three strange emails were waiting for me when I got in this morning. All a little worrying, but I'm sure I can get through it with my positive attitude. The first was from Sarah, warning me that if I come anywhere near the house or try to contact Brad again, it would be a police matter. I replied that I was very sorry about my behaviour, but I'd eaten an out-of-date ready-meal and it had made me violently ill.

The second message was from Trevor, inviting me to another meeting on Monday morning. Now he's got that email to blackmail me with he can make me do what he likes. I'll probably have to go through with the Kit Kat thing this time.

The third email was from Jen. She wants to meet me alone at half eight tomorrow morning. I'm guessing this has something to do with that weird memory I have of snogging her on Saturday night. I expect she's going to sue me for sexual harassment.

All this seems utterly horrendous, but I'm sure it's fine. Everything's absolutely brilliant.

They were having a seventies night in one of the pubs on the high street tonight. I know this because I saw loads of people wearing Afro wigs and bright floral shirts. Unlike any of them, I was alive during the seventies and I seem to remember most people wearing dull nylon shirts and corduroy trousers rather than white satin suits and gold medallions.

If they really want a seventies night, I'll give them one. I'll go in there and induce an authentic seventies power cut. Then when the lights come back on, the lava lamps will be replaced with overflowing bins, the only items on the menu will be mince, spaghetti hoops and Angel Delight, the entire place will be fogged with cigarette smoke and anyone who isn't white, male and heterosexual will have to put up with jokes at their expense all night.

But I'm not going to, because I'm still in positive mode. Must stay positive to avoid mental collapse. Seventies nights are just a harmless bit of fun. I hope they all have a great night dancing to ABBA.

WEDNESDAY 10TH APRIL

Jen was waiting in the meeting room when I got in. She was standing in front of a flipchart and clutching a green marker.

'Sorry,' I said. 'What exactly is this about?'

'It's about what happened on Saturday,' she said.

I sank into the nearest chair. Time for the sexual harassment lawsuit, no doubt.

'Yeah, about that,' I said. 'If you could give me a quick recap of exactly what…'

Jen blushed. 'As you'll be aware, there are a number of options open to us at this point, and I thought we could brainstorm around them.'

She scribbled the words 'Enemies', 'Friends' and 'More' on the flipchart and drew circles around them.

'The first option, which I'm keen to avoid, would be animosity. The second would be to return to the previous S.O.P. and pretend nothing happened. The third option,

which I'm keen to explore, would be to consider other…
things.'

We were silent for a couple of minutes.

'So,' she said. 'Throwing it over to you…'

'I'm slightly confused,' I said. 'Are you asking me out?
With a flipchart?'

Jen bit her bottom lip and nodded.

'Thanks and everything,' I said. 'But the very fact that
you've made the effort to do it this way proves we're too
different. You're efficient and you work hard and you
like everyone whereas I'm a complete fuck-up. But we
can still be option two, can't we?'

It's now one in the morning and I'm really stalling in my efforts to be positive. I feel worse about today than anything I did on Saturday. So what if I made an idiot of myself over a younger girl? Every middle-aged man is allowed to do that once. So what if I threw up on Sarah? I wish I'd done it at the altar. So what if I insulted Trevor? It's not like he didn't deserve it. But I think I really upset Jen today. And she's not a bad person. She's an annoying person, of course. But I'm starting to think she might be rather a nice annoying person.

THURSDAY 11TH APRIL

Jen's typing and muttering got louder and louder all day until eventually she hit her keyboard with both hands, shouted 'Fucking thing!' and ran out of the office. Jez and Jo both folded their arms and looked at me. They seemed to be expecting me to do something about it.

I found Jen standing in the pile of cigarette stubs outside the main entrance. 'I'm fine,' she said. 'I just need a minute.'

'I'm sorry about yesterday,' I said. 'It just freaked me out a bit. With the Venn diagram and everything.'

'It wasn't a Venn diagram,' she said. 'The circles didn't overlap.'

I tried to work out what was different about her voice and I realized she'd stopped talking in questions.

'And I'm not efficient,' she said. 'I'm just as much of a fuck-up as you.'

'Come on,' I said. 'Don't do yourself down.'

'It's true. My flat's even messier than your desk.'

'You're just saying that to impress me.'

'Come round if you don't believe me.'

'All right,' I said. 'Are you free on Saturday?'

FRIDAY 12TH APRIL

Josh called me into his office this afternoon.

'I need a word about the TC Waste Solutions account,' said Josh. 'You'd better close the door.'

I might have known Trevor would grass me up.

'Sorry about that,' I said. 'Someone hacked into my email account. I suspect this guy called Brad.'

'Of what?' asked Josh.

'Nothing,' I said. 'So what did you want to talk about?'

'We've been offered the DDS Waste Solutions account,' said Josh. 'They're the biggest suppliers of industrial bins in the south-east, so it's a great win for us. The trade press are coming round later on to photograph me on the fire escape. The only problem is, they won't give us the business unless we resign the TC Waste Solutions account. Now, I know you've really taken ownership of it…'

206

'I'm happy to sacrifice it,' I said. 'For the sake of our business.'

'Good man,' said Josh. 'I'll call Trevor.'

I pretended to consider this. 'I've got a meeting with him first thing Monday. I could give him the news face to face, if you like. To soften the blow.'

'Excellent call,' said Josh. He held his hand up and this time I high-fived without any hesitation.

SATURDAY 13TH APRIL

I'm a bit nervous about going round to Jen's flat tonight. I'm not sure I want to try anything with her in case she gets her flipchart out afterwards and gives me a formal appraisal.

Having said that, I'm nowhere near as terrified as I usually am before a date. I'm just trying to get round to laying the decking and watching my *Sopranos* box set like usual. It makes a change from my usual self-fulfilling prophecies of disaster and humiliation.

SUNDAY 14TH APRIL

Jen's flat was exactly the kind of tip she'd promised. She lives on the top floor of a house conversion, with Paul Klee prints Blu-Tacked over damp patches and fairy lights twirled around metal shelves. Everywhere I went I seemed to knock over a pile of handbag-sized magazines with cumbersome free gifts or novels with champagne flutes on the cover. I made her promise she hadn't deliberately messed it up for me, and cleared myself a space to sit down.

When I first met Jen, I'd imagined that she lived in a penthouse apartment with a river view, a chrome kitchen island, and a focus group employed to give 24-hour feedback. But now this mess seemed to make sense.

Even I wasn't prepared for the lasagne, though.

'This is brilliant,' I said.

Jen looked puzzled. 'Really? People don't often compliment me on my cooking.'

'I wasn't complimenting you on your cooking,' I said. 'It's horrible. But the fact it's horrible proves that you weren't lying about being as shambolic as me. No one truly efficient or professional could ever have made this. That's what's brilliant.'

Monday 15th April

When I got to Trevor's office this morning, he was sitting behind his desk and grasping a yellow tennis ball.

'I take it you were under the influence when you wrote that email?' he asked.

'Yeah,' I said. 'Sorry.'

'Well, I will hold it against you,' he said. 'But I won't tell Josh. Not if you play ball.'

He threw the ball at me. It bounced off my forehead and back on to his desk, and I rubbed the spot it had hit.

'Fifty points,' he shouted.

'What?'

'Don't tell me you don't remember "Trevor Chalkley Dodgeball",' he said. 'You invented it. Everyone had to throw a tennis ball at me and I had to try and dodge it. You got ten points for hitting my arms or legs, twenty for hitting my body and fifty for hitting my head.'

I picked up the ball.

'I do remember it,' I said. 'But I thought the rules were different. I thought you got a hundred points for this.'

I threw the ball at his face. He ducked out of the way, but his chair overbalanced and he crashed to the floor.

210

When he got up again, his face was red. 'That's it! The account's walking! I'm going to call Josh right now and tell him it's all your fault.'

'Yeah, about that,' I said. 'I regret to inform you that we've been awarded the DDS Waste Solutions account so we're going to have to resign this one. But I'd like to take this opportunity to thank you for working with us and wish you all the best for the future.'

'DDS?' asked Trevor. 'You can't work for those crooks. They won't pay you, you know. They'll leave your invoices lying around for years.'

'I'm afraid the decision has already been taken,' I said.

'What are they paying you?' Trevor asked. 'I'll match it.'

'You couldn't afford it,' I said. 'DDS are the biggest industrial bin suppliers in the south-east. Bar none.'

I walked out of the office, and Trevor came scurrying after me.

'Get back here,' he shouted.

I kept walking. Some of Trevor's staff poked their heads out of their offices.

'This meeting isn't over until I say it is!' shouted Trevor.

I felt something whip me on the back of my arm.

'Ten points!'

I turned round to see that Trevor was lobbing whiteboard markers at me from a box. A crowd had gathered behind him, and some of them were filming it with their phones.

'Twenty points!' he shouted. 'Fifty points! A million points! I win! Because I'm a winner and you're a loser!'

'Course you are,' I said. 'Course you are, Chalky Balls.'

Tuesday 16th April

Josh briefed me on the DDS Waste Solutions account today. There's a lot to do in a short time, but I'm determined to get through it. I'm going to write a bin brochure so brilliant that all Trevor's clients will switch their business right away and he'll go bust. That's got to be worth working through lunch for.

I went out for a drink with Jen again after work. We're trying to keep it secret from everyone in the office, but it's not exactly difficult for them to guess. Jo complained about Jen's muttering this afternoon, and I said it was hardly surprising if she was stressed, as she was doing more work than the rest of us put together. Jo and Jez looked at each other, did a childish 'woo' noise and burst out laughing.

I'm sure those youngsters find middle age hilarious and disgusting, but they'll know all about it soon. It won't be long before they find themselves grunting when they pick things up, going to the chemist's just to browse and discovering strange new facial hairs whenever they look in the mirror. And then some smug little bastards will park themselves on the desk next to them and snigger whenever they mention ridiculously antiquated stuff like Facebook or Starbucks.

Go ahead and laugh, kids. You'll be here soon.

Wednesday 17th April

I was all set to work through lunch when Jen suggested we go to the Italian restaurant around the corner. I thought about my plan to work hard enough to put Trevor out of business and then I thought about pizza. There was no contest really. I'll take food over revenge any day.

When we got to the restaurant, Jen ordered the chicken pesto salad, but requested so many changes to it that she might as well have barged into the kitchen and made it herself. I'm always wary about suggesting changes to chefs. Catch them on a bad day and you'll find that a side order of phlegm is the only modification you get. They didn't seem to mind Jen, though. She actually smiles and looks at waiters when she speaks to them, which seems to result in much better service. It's not something I've ever really tried.

I should have got her to ask them to turn off the background music, which was annoying me. It wasn't that it was good or bad, it was just inconsistent. In the old days, an Italian restaurant would play a CD of Pavarotti or Dean Martin all the way through. These days all restaurant staff just hook their iPods up to the speakers and put them on shuffle. So today we had pop, opera and rock all jumbled up. It was only the Fellini posters and breadsticks that reminded me what sort of restaurant it was.

I managed to ignore it and told Jen about my workload on the DDS account. She said she'd take on some of the work if I wanted. It's weird. I used to think she worked hard just to crawl to Josh. Now I know her better, I'm convinced she actually enjoys it, in the way that a normal person might enjoy eating pies or watching TV.

Should I ask Josh if she can take over some of my work? I want to, but I don't think it's acceptable to ask your boss for less work these days. It's like drinking pints at lunchtime. You just don't do it any more.

215

When the bill came, I noticed they'd done that annoying thing of adding a service charge to the total and also leaving a space for a 'gratuity'. Are 'service charge' and 'gratuity' different things now? Would you like a tip as well? How about I just hand over my wallet and you grab money out of it until it's all right for me to stop feeling awkward?

I suggested to Jen that we cross the service charge off the bill and put nothing in the gratuity section, but she said the waiters were such 'sweeties' that she didn't mind paying both. Probably another reason her food doesn't get gobbed in.

216

When I got back in the office, Josh asked if I could keep my desk tidier. He said it will make things easier when we all start hotdesking. I was hoping he'd forgotten about that and moved on to some other voguish nonsense like constructing a breakout beanbag brainstorming area in the corner of the office. I can't have my screen facing away from the wall. That would be unbearable.

THURSDAY 18TH APRIL

I bumped into my old boss Steve after work tonight. It turns out the old fart is off snorkelling on the Great Barrier Reef. I hope they don't mistake him for an ancient undiscovered species of turtle and stick him in an aquarium.

I thanked him for telling Josh I was a good worker and he almost collapsed with laughter.

'A good worker?' he said. 'Is that what he told you?'

'I thought it was a bit strange,' I said. 'What with me being a lazy sod and everything. So why did you suggest that he keep me rather than Imran or Cathy?'

'I didn't,' said Steve. 'But it doesn't really matter what I or anyone else suggests, the company can't afford to get rid of you. You've been there for over fifteen years.

Have you any idea how much redundancy pay they'd owe you? I tried to manage you out by reducing your workload so much you'd feel unfulfilled and go, but it never worked. You'll be there until the place closes, I'm sure.'

'Thanks,' I said. 'I think.'

Friday 19th April

Josh came over this morning to ask how I was getting on with the DDS brochure.

'Not great,' I said. 'I think I need an extra week.'

'An extra week?' asked Josh. 'To do 2,000 words?'

'Yeah,' I said. 'In fact, make it a fortnight. And I've been thinking about the hotdesking thing, too. I don't want to do it. I'm happy where I am.'

Josh tutted, shook his head and went back to his office. I saved and closed my Word document. After all, that Scrabble was hardly going to play itself, was it?

We went out to the Italian restaurant for lunch again. This time Jen changed her order about twenty minutes after giving it, but still the waiters didn't seem to mind.

'Can I ask you a question?'

My neck tensed up. She wasn't one of those women
that talks about marriage after just a week, was she?

'Go on,' I said.

'How soon did you know you were interested in me?'

'About five seconds after I saw you.'

Jen blushed and looked down at her cutlery. I didn't feel guilty because technically I wasn't lying. I did fancy her five seconds after I saw her. It was only when she started speaking that I became less interested, and that would be incredibly hard to explain during a romantic meal.

'So you can guess my next question,' said Jen. 'What took you so long to make a move after I sent you the Valentine's card?'

SATURDAY 20TH APRIL

I went into town with Jen this afternoon. She dragged me around a million clothes shops, and then into a place that sold nothing but soap. They had honey soap, fig soap and even something called 'sea vegetable'. The pong of it all was worse than any body odour could ever be, and I had to go and wait outside while Jen browsed.

For some reason, it didn't make me grumpy. All day I encountered things that should have made me grind my teeth down to tiny white stumps, like buskers, tourists and charity muggers, but I didn't mind at all. What's going wrong with me? Maybe I've finally taken one of those 'chill pills' that Jez is always going on about. Maybe he slipped one into my tea.

After Jen had accumulated an armful of carrier bags, we walked slowly down the street and popped into Starbucks. I waited in the queue while Jen dashed over to grab the last remaining free sofa. The man in front of me, who was on his own, turned round and scowled.

I had to order Jen a 'Grande skinny mocha Frapuccino with no cream' and I didn't even feel like punching myself in the face. Something very odd is going on.

SUNDAY 21ST APRIL

I saw that little kid who stole my phone this morning. He was sitting on a bench and playing a hip hop track through the speakers of it. Not only was he inflicting his horrendous tastes on everyone, but he was doing it with something that didn't belong to him. I should have held him in a headlock until the police arrived, but I couldn't be bothered. Why not let him have the phone? He looked like he was getting a lot more enjoyment out of it than I ever did. I even found myself smiling and saying 'good morning' as I passed.

He looked up at me and shielded his eyes from the sun. 'Piss off, you paedo,' he said, before turning his attention back to the phone.

Ah, the younger generation. What a pleasant place this world will be when they're in charge.

As you might have guessed, I'm going out with Jen now. I know the phrase 'going out' makes us sound like teenagers snogging in a bus shelter, but I can't think of a better one. I could say we're boyfriend and girlfriend, but I'm not a boy any more and she's not a girl, though she looks a lot younger than me. I could say we're 'in a relationship' but that sounds too formal, and brings back horrendous memories of serious discussions with Sarah.

So here's the thing. I started writing this diary to see how long I could stick with it. And to my surprise, I kept it going for almost four months. But it contains a number of unfortunate remarks about Jen, based on my misguided first impressions. I don't want her to see them, so I'm going to read this diary through once more, then take it out into the garden and burn it. And after that I'm going to get on with the decking and watch my *Sopranos* box set.

I was just about to start reading the diary again when I got some new Facebook notifications. Jen has tagged us in some photos she took yesterday. An old friend who I haven't seen for years commented, 'I can't believe how great Sarah looks in these – even better than she did when I knew you!!! Lucky bastard.'

God, I hope Sarah saw that.

223

I've read the diary through again and I think it's time to put it out of its misery. Looks like I won't be recording my gripes for the rest of the year, although I'm guessing that summer will be too wet and Christmas decorations will go on sale too early. I doubt I'll miss it, though. I've already done enough ranting for one year.